Surviving The Forest
Adiva Geffen

My thoughts and admiration to the wondrous people who survived the terrors of the Holocaust and went on to create a new life and share their stories of triumph with me. This book is a reflection of their fortitude.

My friend, Arlyn Roffman, who gracefully and professionally accompanied me during the translation process and added her magic touch.

Greatest thanks to Zoe who gave this book soul and spirit in English. Her accuracy, guidance and honesty is deeply appreciated.

Surviving The Forest
Adiva Geffen

Copyright © 2019 Adiva Geffen

Translation: Zoe Jordan
Contact: adivageffen@gmail.com

ISBN 9789655750102

SURVIVING THE FOREST

Adiva Geffen

OUT OF THE FOREST

Quiet, quiet, let's be silent.
Death is growing here.
It was planted by the tyrant, See its bloom appear.
All the roads lead to Paneri now,
There is no route back,
And our father too has vanished,
And with him our light.
Shush, my child, don't cry, my gem.
Tears will never help,
Our enemy will
Never understand...

"Ponary" Shmerke Kaczerginski

One sees and achieves only once: as a child.

*The first sights are the first sources of imagery that accompany
you all your life, and all the sights that come after are but
inferior pictures. Your first home is a mirror of your life
and you will love it to the depths of your soul. Sometimes
the memory surrounds you and appears clear and pure, and
sometimes it appears stuttering and vague. But there is always
that spirit that wishes to return to the first home, to the
memory of childhood, to the sounds and smells where we knew
happiness and felt forever safe. Life's tumult cannot silence the
voices of longing.*

*Memory will always take me back to the village, to the kitchen
where Mama is making dumplings, and I'm there, beside the
window, drinking in the sights.*

—Haim Nachman Bialik

⚜

This is the story of a woman called Sarah, who made it out of the forest, where the graves of her fallen loved ones would forever remain.

Sarah, who left the forest and came into the light and back to life.

There are many ways to begin her story.

Maybe like in an old fairy tale.

"Once upon a time there was a beautiful woman who had a loving husband and a gorgeous daughter and one day..." Or we could try, "Many years ago, long before the whole world was turned upside down by the terrible war that annihilated and devoured everything and in which millions of people died or were murdered..."

But in this case we will begin the story in the days when people were happy with their lot and thanked God for all He had given them.

"In a little village, not far from the town of Ostrow Lubelski and the Parczew Forest, happily lived the Shidlovsky family. Father Yaakov Mendel and Mother Taiba."

Beside their house spread a green field where they grew vegetables and wheat and a beautiful flower garden. In the yard stood apple and pear trees and a small stream that ran between them. Chickens ran about the yard, along with five goats and two cows, their udders full of milk.

Yaakov Mendel and Taiba Shidlovsky saw that their work was blessed and rejoiced and hoped that their home would be filled with children. They saw blessings in everything they had and were thankful for the abundance and the goodness. In their little house at the crossroads, they would fall asleep in each other's arms, with a smile on their lips, in their bed, under a soft quilt, thankful to God for all He had granted them.

But in contrast to happier fairy tales and fables, our story has a different plot.

Somewhere, at the edge of the skies, Satan awoke and looked upon this family. It hurt him to see their little bit of happiness of those people and the little house in the village of Taiba and Yaakov Mendel in Eastern Poland. Across the mountains and the great forests, he made his plans to spread his treacherous fingers through their beautiful country, into the fields and meadows, the thick forests and the green valleys... deep into the serene villages where clear water flowed. Even God, to whom people appealed for assistance, would not be able to help them.

Meanwhile in their little house, Yaakov Mendel and Taiba fell asleep in their bed, and dreamed their dreams. Little did they know that somewhere to the west, evil plans were already being hatched and many dark clouds were quickly moving east.

1.

The house of Yaakov Mendel and Taiba Shidlovsky stood on the eastern side of the small Polish village of Wolka Zablocka. It was a peaceful village, inhabited for hundreds of years by farmers who worked the land. Although there were not many people, there was affection and friendship among its inhabitants, Jews and Gentiles alike. They lived alongside one another in the village in amicable harmony.

The Jews lived their lives as Poles but kept up the Jewish traditions at home; they made sure to observe the Sabbath, to fast on Yom Kippur, and build sukkahs on Sukkot to which they would invite their neighbors. On Hanukkah they lit the menorah candles, and on Passover they sat around the Seder table with their relatives from the neighboring villages, or would go to celebrate the holidays with their families in the neighboring town of Ostrow Lubelski. The Jews of the small village made sure to invite their Gentile neighbors to the holidays and family events to celebrate with them, and made an effort to visit the Christians in their homes to celebrate on their holidays.

If outsiders were to visit the village, they would not have been able to tell if the milkman they met was a Jew who prayed facing east, or a Christian who believed in Jesus Christ. "We are all farmers working our land, regardless of religion or race," the village mayor, Stefan Sznetski would certainly have said. "The Jews are my brothers; my mother died in childbirth, and

Rachel the Jew nursed my brother and me. We always called her 'Mamushka Rachel.'"

How could Stefan have known that only a few years later, when the first Germans arrived to the region and began to sniff around to get to know the territory, it would be his own drunken son, Lucien, the village good-for-nothing, who had suffered badly in his youth, who would rush to the German headquarters in Lublin and offer his services - particularly his knowledge of who was "one of us" and who was not, in exchange for being appointed village mayor?

In Wolka Zablocka, there was a little wooden hut in which two families lived, one next to the other. On the right side of the hut, facing the Parczew Forest, lived the childless Uncle Yaakov Mendel and Aunt Alinka, and on the other side, facing the path which led to the village center, lived Yaakov Mendel and Taiba, the parents of Shurka. People of the village affectionately called them, "our two Yaakov Mendels."

The hut was covered with a red-tiled roof, evergreen ivy that climbed up the front, and rosebushes, clinging to the hut walls and adorning the little house with red flowers, lovingly tended by Taiba. The walls were thick with double windows, which were necessary to protect its inhabitants against the bitter cold of Poland's snowy winters. The house overlooked green fields; from it one could see the routes leading to the neighboring villages and the nearby town of Ostrow Lubelski, only several kilometers away, where a larger community of Jews had resided since the middle of the 17th century.

From there one could see the window of the house of Chaya Bila, the sister of Taiba who lived up the road. To the north, the path led to Kolano and next to them, on a broad open field, lived the Poznansky family, headed by the village shoemaker who was a close friend of Yaakov Mendel. East of the house, a path stretched north, to the large estate of Fritz Luboskowitz, who was admired and respected by all the villagers. Fritz Luboskowitz has an important role in our story.

If you had been invited to the house in those days, it is safe to assume that you would were warmly received. On summer days Taiba would serve her guests freshly squeezed lemonade and in the winter she would sit them on a bench beside the stove so they could warm up and rest from the hardships of the road. Taiba would be pleased if, between servings of fish and challah, her guests would tell her what was happening in their own nearby villages: who had gotten married, who had gotten sick (God forbid), who had given birth or (God forbid) who had died. In those days there was radio to bring the news, but it was a rare thing in the villages, and only Fritz had one in his home. Traveling salesmen would bring the news, which spread through their gossip among the villages.

In the center of the hut beside the large dining table stood an ancient bookcase made of walnut, whose shelves were crammed with books. *Legends of Chazal, "Shulchan Aruch,"* a prayer book for Shabbat and the holidays, copies of the Bible, the *Gemara*, the *Tseno Ureno*, and other holy books illustrated with special pictures. They had been handed down from their parents or purchased from the owner of the wagon that passed through the villages selling holy books.

If their house were ever touched by the fingers of the devil, the family would try with all their might to defend and to save those books. But in the meantime, there were blue skies overhead, and they would read and enjoy them on both the special and routine days of their lives.

Beside the bookshelf stood the cupboard in which the

Passover plates, Taiba's dowry, were stored and locked away. There was glass and crystalware, silver that had been passed down for many generations, Kiddush cups, Shabbat candleholders which came from Yaakov Mendel's parents and, of course, an ornate cup for Elijah the prophet. On top of the cupboard was a big wooden box which held the paper decorations for the sukkah. A small box was placed there too. This one contained Taiba's jewelry: ruby earrings, gold bracelets, and a pearl necklace she wore to family celebrations or trips to visit her parents and relatives.

Like most of the villagers, Yaakov Mendel was also a farmer who made his living off the property that he rented from Fritz. He diligently managed the small family plot. In autumn he plowed the fields, in the spring he sowed the seeds, and at the end of summer he would harvest. In the mornings he took his small herd out to graze, milked the cows and the goats by hand, and worked over the big fields with his horse-drawn plow. Taiba helped him, scattering grain for the chickens, gathering the eggs, making cheese from the milk or churning it into butter. They sold some of their products to their neighbors or to merchants passing through the village, but most of it was intended for consumption by the family, which grew with the arrival of their firstborn daughter, Sarah.

As soon as she was born, Taiba announced that she should be called Sarah. "Why?" Everyone asked her. Taiba said because she loves Sarah, our foremother who was beautiful, smart and beloved, "and perhaps my Sarah will also be blessed with her own sort of Abraham." They nicknamed her Shurka - Shurka the beautiful.

Upon the arrival of the new baby, all of the villagers came to congratulate the happy family. Their Christian friends, believers of Jesus Christ, crossed themselves before the baby and said a blessing, paying their respects with fresh eggs and the best seeds. Their Jewish friends brought wine and thanked the God of Abraham, Isaac, and Jacob for this parcel of joy, and a stream of relatives came from the neighboring villages to see the beautiful Shurka and deliver their gifts to her.

Shurka was indeed an unusually beautiful and intelligent baby.

"Also pretty and also smart," said Aunt Alinka.

"Most importantly, she's such a happy girl," said the proud Taiba.

"Even more important that she should be lucky," said Lyudmila, the shoemaker's wife, and crossed herself.

Shurka was beloved by everyone in her family. Her honey-colored hair spilled over her shoulders in waves, her voice was as clear as a bell, she smelled of dates, and her laughter would roll from one end of the hut to the other. When she grew and learned to walk, she would run freely around the yard among the animals. Her parents would watch her proudly, glowing with happiness.

When she turned two, her grandmother, Irena, Yaakov Mendel's mother, moved into their home. Her father went to the nearby Ostrow Lubelski, where Irena lived with her late husband who ran a small tailor shop. Papa harnessed the wagon and went to bring her, and when they returned the following day, he called out loudly, "Shurka, Taiba, come come, Grandma is here!" and helped her down from the wagon. Her face was forlorn. Slowly she got off the wagon and let out a big sigh.

"Why is she so sad?" asked Shurka, and hid behind her mother's apron.

"Because her life is hard," whispered her mother.

"Why?" Shurka prodded.

"Because she is alone."

"Why?"

"Questions, questions, go hug your grandmother."

Shurka hurried to hug her grandmother who immediately burst into tears, "Oy me, oy my life, oy, oy!"

"Look Mama, she isn't even happy to see us." Shurka hid behind Taiba who wiped a tear from her cheek and said yes, she is very happy to see us, but she is also sad because she misses her husband, your Saba."

"Why?"

"Questions, questions! Go hug her." She prodded Shurka who was holding the edge of her dress, "Saba passed away and left Grandma alone. She will live with us."

"Why is she alone?" Shurka asks.

But her mother answered, "Enough, better you should show Grandma around the house."

"Now, Shurka," said Papa, who was putting her to sleep, "you must look after Grandma. From now on she will live with us."

"I am glad she is with us," whispered Shurka. "Just so you know, she is not crying as much anymore."

Shurka hugged her grandmother and inhaled the scent of yeast embedded in her clothes. She loved the cakes her grandmother baked for them.

When Grandma moved in with them, the house filled with the smells of new dishes. She knew how to make cabbage stuffed with veal, aromatic vegetable pies, and sweet challah bread. On winter evenings, Grandma would place a packet of wool in Shurka's small hands and roll it into one big ball from, which she would knit warm vests and winter hats for the members of the household. "How nice it is that Grandma is here," said little Shurka and Grandma gave her chocolate cake that she called rogelach.

When winter came and with it the snowstorms which covered the house, Grandma asked to move to her brother's home in Ostrow Lubelski. So Papa harnessed the horses again, hooked up the wagon and Grandma departed.

"I will return in the spring," she promised Shurka who sobbed bitterly, "like the storks."

That same year, many days before the soldiers of the Third Reich marched in their boots and trampled Poland, long before the clouds of the war began to gather in the west, the family decided to set out on a journey and move to Israel, the renewed homeland.

They had heard from their friends and guests that Jews were beginning to return there. The old homeland was destroyed and abandoned and was in need of hard-toiling people like them who would plow and sow the earth and work the land that God promised to Abraham, and make the two-thousand-year-old wilderness bloom.

They so hoped to move that they had already considered changing their family name to the Hebraic *Shamir* or *Shalom*. They dreamed and dreamed and wondered whether they would prefer the mountains in the north or the central plain. But their dream would never come to fruition.

"Everything could have been different if only... if only..." Shurka later reflected, her blue eyes saddening. "It's a shame. We surely would have moved to Israel if we had not heard the stories of the hardship that awaited us there, if Papa hadn't worried about us, if... If... But man cannot predict how his decisions will affect his life and the lives of those dear to him. Everyone just tries to do their best." She still remembered the excitement that gripped the small family. After all, they planned to go off on a journey, to the land of their forefathers, somewhere across the sea. This was no trivial matter.

Two young recruiters from the Eretz Israel came to encourage them to leave Poland and go to the Holy Land. In the eyes of little Shurka, they appeared so different from Papa, from her uncles, and all the people that she knew from the village. Their skin was tanned and brown, they wore strange clothes and no hats on their heads, and most of all, they spoke the language that she recognized from prayers. They brought with them a fruit, orange in color, which she had never seen before. They said it was a 'golden apple.'

It was already evening and the foreigners were sitting in the small kitchen telling story after story of this other land, the listeners all thirstily gulping their words.

Sometimes they would burst out singing in a funny language, show her family photographs of a small lake that they called the Sea of Galilee and of strange trees that they called palm trees, the likes of which she had never seen. Shurka did not know this faraway place that they called by strange names like the 'land of Zion,' 'land of our fathers,' sometimes 'Jerusalem,' and sometimes 'our old homeland.'

"Is it far, the old homeland?" She tugged at her father's pants.

"Very far," smiled Papa Yaakov Mendel. "You must take a train and then a boat. Soon enough we will all travel to the Land of Israel."

"Papa, what is the Land of Israel?" Shurka asked. "We are

Poles, why do you call it our homeland?"

"Because that is our true homeland."

"What is a homeland?"

"It is the place where our forefathers and mothers lived: Abraham, Isaac, and Jacob. And Sarah and Rivka," said Taiba.

Papa explained to her that Jerusalem was the place where the Jews dreamed of returning, that it was very far away, across the sea. It was the place where the storks flew for the cold winter, where the sun warms and the seashore is white and fresh. He even let her taste a piece of the juicy orange fruit that never grew on their tree.

"This is called an orange, or a 'golden apple.'" her father told her excitedly. "And there, in Israel, there are many golden fruits."

"Why did they bring us the apple?"

"Remember my little Shurka, this is an orange, a '*golden* apple.' They brought it here to show us how fertile the land of Zion is. There, in the land of our fathers, they are beginning to rebuild the old homeland. The people building it are called pioneers."

"What is a pioneer?"

"My curious girl! They are the first to return and begin to build it up again. And they need farmers like me, people who know how to plow the land, to grow apples and to milk cows. People with hands like mine. See, look," said Yaakov Mendel and raised his strong hands and stroked Shurka's head. "Our friend Moshe Yanovsky, who lived in the neighboring village, has already gone. He will be a pioneer and then it will be our turn."

"And do they speak Polish there, like here?"

"No," answered the aunt. "We will have to learn a new

language."

"Which?"

"The language is called 'Hebrew,'" said Taiba.

"Hebrew is the language of our prayers and now they are revising and modernizing it, like the earth, like our people... the Jewish people."

Uncle Yaakov Mendel and Aunt Alinka also wanted to come on the journey. They too dreamed of building a new life in the land of the forefathers. They too wanted to work the earth of the homeland.

"Wonderful," laughed Taiba. "The whole family will live all together again."

"Of course," said Uncle Yaakov Mendel, "all of us in one house, of one heart, in peace and love."

"Amen, Amen."

Mama began to prepare for the voyage with great excitement. She sewed sheets and embroidered tablecloths, and even put some of the furniture up for sale.

And Papa taught them how to say 'water' and 'milk' and 'cheese' and 'thank you' in Hebrew.

"Mah-yeem, maa-eem," Shurka tried to pronounce the new word in Hebrew, which made everyone laugh.

Shurka repeated the funny words and at night she would recite them to her soft cloth doll Alinka, which she had received as a birthday gift. She would teach her the new words she had learned because very soon, she explained, they would speak a different language in a different country. In the evenings, Papa would tell them of the forefathers who had lived in Israel, of Sarah and Rachel, of King David and the Temple that stood on top of the mountains. This land had golden sand dunes and golden apples and palm trees. Shurka was fascinated by the stories of Abraham, Isaac, and Jacob, and of Joseph and his brothers. She had already begun to dream of that faraway place, the Land of Israel. Only Grandma Irena was grumbling in her room. She did not understand what that land had that could not be found here.

"After all, Poland is our homeland," she kept saying but Papa would tell her that to immigrate to the land of the forefathers was a big dream. A dream that must be realized.

But then rumors began to arrive in that little village in Eastern Poland about the old homeland.

One day a carriage drawn by two horses pulled up beside the hut of Taiba and Yaakov Mendel and their neighbor, Moshe Yanovsky, got down from it. He was thinner than they remembered, and his face was red. Taiba peered from the window then hurried out to greet him.

"Moshe Yanovsky, what are you doing here? I thought that you were all there, in the Land of Israel."

"As you see I am back here in our Wolka Zablocka," answered Moshe sadly.

"Did something happen?"

He did not answer, but only asked where he could find the two Yaakov Mendel. Taiba understood right away. She nodded her head and sent Shurka to call her father to come quick. When the two Yaakov Mendel heard who their guest was, they immediately stopped their milking and hurried to the house.

"Hurrah, Yanovsky the hero!" they called him from afar, waving their hands in greeting.

Soon cries of joy were replaced with cries of sorrow and with every word that Moshe Yanovsky uttered, Yaakov Mendel's face reddened.

"We must go there, in spite of everything," he said loudly in his powerful voice.

"But how? You heard what he said," Uncle Yaakov protested, having already begun to pull back from the plans.

"And yet we will immigrate to Israel."

"You are a crazy man," said Yanovsky. "People are dropping like flies from malaria."

"In spite of everything, despite the malaria outbreak there, though there is no work and the earth is hard and treacherous," he laughed, "it's our homeland! They need people like us, working men."

"True, but perhaps it is better that you wait a little," said Moshe Yanovsky. "Maybe it is not yet time."

"How long shall we wait?" asked Yaakov Mendel. "We already have the travel papers and permissions, and who knows what will be. We must take action, not wait. We must rebuild our homeland."

Papa Yaakov Mendel was stubborn and insisted that they must go, even though Taiba and Aunt Alinka were worried. They said that maybe Moshe was right, that maybe it would be better to wait until the situation became more stable.

"Our Shurka is still small," said Taiba, "let's wait a little - what's wrong with that?!"

"We've waited for two thousand years, we can wait two more," added Aunt Alinka.

Yaakov Mendel went out to the yard and paced, with a serious expression and a furrowed brow. He rolled one of the thin cigarillos that he allowed himself from time to time. Moshe Yanovsky and Uncle Yaakov Mendel stood silently watching him.

Taiba went out to him. They talked and they talked for a long time, and when he came back, his eyes were sad and his smile was gone.

The next morning, the two Yaakov Mendel announced that they had decided to forgo their plans for the time being.

"Just for now," emphasized Papa.

"What happened?" Shurka asked her mother.

"Didn't you hear?!" her father grumbled and she disappeared behind her mother's apron.

"It's over. It was decided that we aren't going," Taiba told her daughter, with sadness in her eyes, "just for the time being."

"Why?" Shurka insisted, "You said it is good there, that it is warm and nice and there are golden apples."

"Because they say it is not yet time." Yaakov Mendel waved his hand towards the broad fields, pointed at the flower garden and said: "For now we will remain here, until there, in the land of our forefathers, the conditions change. I do not want my family to starve, heaven forbid. Let's wait. Maybe the time truly is not right yet."

Many years later, when Shurka arrived in the Land of Israel, and everyone called her Grandma Shurka, she would tell her grandchildren, "Papa believed that within one year, we would pack and sell all of our things, and go to Israel. Maybe even two years when we could be sure that the homeland was ready for us, he promised. And we waited patiently. We believed him that we would still get there, and after all, it was good for us in Poland in those days. How could we have known..."

The days passed by swiftly, until Shurka was four years old. Her favorite place in her parents' home was the kitchen window, with its bright blue curtain covered in embroidered red and blue forest flowers. She could sit there for hours, squeezed in next to the two double-paned windows, and look out at the world opening up before her. Even now, after all the years that have passed, Shurka remembers the sights. They are a part of her. They are the album of her childhood memories. From that vantage point she would watch the snow fall, the flowers of frost bloom on the windows, the fields becoming green in the spring, and caress the rays of the sun where they met the glass. She loved to observe. She consumed the world through her eyes.

"Look Mama," she exclaimed, trying to grasp the sunlight in her hands. "It's so pretty," she rejoiced, and her mother hugged her and whispered to her daughter that she too, once loved watching and observing, to hold those beautiful images of the world in her heart.

"And, if God wills it, so too will your children and your children's children," Taiba silently prayed.

"This is the best place in the world, right Mama?"

"Exactly."

How could they have known that the day would come when all that remained of their pretty wooden house, which was home to that happiness, would be a handful of ash? That a wicked hand would wipe from the face of the earth all that was built with love. How was it possible, in the face of all this beauty, to know how much evil there is in the world?

Our little Shurka loved to press her face against the cold glass window, to wave with her small hands to the village children returning from school and throwing their schoolbags into the air, to call Papa and Uncle Yaakov Mendel as they went about their work: giving grains of wheat to the chickens, brushing the horses, milking the cows, weeding, plowing the fields or seeding onions and carrots.

"Papa, look at me, I'm here!" she called and Papa would set

down the buckets he was holding and smile at her, wipe the sweat from his face and continue with his work. Sometimes he would come to the window and hand her a pea pod or a chestnut flower.

Mama Taiba would be busy in the kitchen, her quick hands dancing over the blue oilcloth on the table, hurrying to prepare supper for the family. She would crush the fresh head of cabbage she had picked from the garden from which she made the sour salad and decorate it with slices of carrot. She would cut up the squash and the onion and stir them in the big soup pot, and churn cheese and sour cream from the milk that Yaakov Mendel brought her. Taiba would beat the ball of dough, until it was soft and flexible, then roll it out and cut broad circles from it. In the center of each circle she would place potatoes and onion, skillfully close its edges and throw it into boiling water. And when Mama was busy, Shurka would drag the wooden chair, which was taller than she was, climb carefully up onto it and from there onto the wooden cupboard. Beside her she would place Alinka. She would fold her little legs on the wooden board, press her head against the cool windowpane and look out at the big pear tree which grew right in front, its heavy branches swaying in the wind, stroking the walls of the house. Little Shurka was sure that it was dancing just for her, bowing for her in a strange way and gesturing for her to come out and climb it.

"Enough, my girl, time to get down," Mama Taiba would pull at Shurka. "It's cold there, come sit beside me, and bring your doll Alinka. Maybe you will get to try some of the beet soup I made."

Shurka pulled herself away from the window, jumping off the cupboard into Taiba's arms. She told her mother about the wind that brought the black clouds and scattered the pile of straw, and about the pear tree that had beautified itself with white flowers.

"Enough idling - better you should help me knead," laughed Mama, as she pushed a piece of soft dough into her daughter's hands, showing her how to roll it into a ball and throw it into the pot of boiling water. Alinka the doll received her own tiny ball of dough. Afterwards, Mama handed Shurka a small basket, and the two carefully gathered eggs from the chicken coop, placing them in the pantry beside the kitchen. They sold some of the eggs to other farmers in exchange for apples or flour.

Twice a year, on the days leading up to Passover and Rosh Hashana, the Jewish New Year, the glass trader's wagon would arrive to their house in the village. Motel Shidlovsky was Taiba's cousin.

When he neared the house he would call out, "Hey, Hello Cousin!" and Taiba would run to him, offer him a hot meal and get the family news: who got engaged and who married, who was expecting a child or had just had one.

"And this is for the prettiest cousin in Poland," Motel Shidlovsky would say and present Taiba with one of the dishes from the factory where he worked, the biggest glass factory of the town of Berzo. The happy Taiba would examine the new dish and place it among the glassware set aside for special occasions.

"Maybe you would like to stay the night in our home?" Taiba would offer but he always had to rush off. There were many more villages yet to visit.

"See you again at Passover!" Motel would shout as he sped

the horses along.

Other guests would visit the house. Taiba would often stop the cloth merchant who came from Ostrow Lubelski or the trader of pots and pans from Parczew and the merchant would ask, "Hello Jews, how are we today. Is Mr. Yaakov Mendel at home?"

"Which Mr. Yaakov Mendel are you looking for?" Taiba would ask.

"And how many Yaakov Mendels are there here?"

"Just two," replied Taiba, laughing.

Taiba was all laughter and joy while Aunt Alinka was bitter and sad. From morning until evening she would scour and clean her home and scold the neighbors' children who played beside the house or sang in the field just across from them. There was a heaviness about her, with her severe face and her hard eyes. The children would see her approaching and scatter in every direction.

"Mama," said Shurka, "did you know that Aunt Alinka is sometimes like the evil witch from the stories you tell me?" And Taiba would caress and calm her.

"You should not speak that way about her."

"But she—"

"You must understand, Aunt Alinka has no children of her own. She is gruff but inside she is sad. She does not have a lovely princess like I have."

In the evenings Papa Yaakov Mendel would bring the cows back from pasture and hurry them into the yard. After finishing various farm duties the family would go into the little kitchen. Papa would read from his book and Mama would serve dinner and then gather her little girl into her lap and tell her all sorts of stories: of golden fish, princesses and witches, hungry wolves and brave children.

***

As the days grew shorter, and the cold winds began to blow, the storks disappeared from the big nest they had built at the top of the electric pole.

"Mama!" cried Shurka, "Look, the nest is gone. What happened to my storks? Who took them?"

"Nobody took the storks, my sweet girl," laughed Taiba. "They simply went away on a long journey."

Shurka looked at her mother in surprise. "Journey? The storks went on a train?"

"They flew."

"Where did they fly?"

"Far away from here. They flew to warmer places, where they grow oranges and palm trees, like you saw in the books that the pioneers left."

"Please, Mama," Shurka pleaded, "ask them to come back soon."

"Don't worry," laughed Taiba. "They will return to us in the springtime, as they do every year. They will clean out their nest and lay eggs, and chicks will hatch and you, my sweet girl, can bring them water and seeds."

And more time passed and Shurka was six years old. She wore two braids and a blue ribbon in her hair. On one of the first days of spring, the sun rose high in the sky, shining on the petals of the flowers that had bloomed in the yard and lighting up the big fields. After the snow in the window had melted, Shurka could return to her favorite spot, and look out at the world.

"Come, my little one," Yaakov Mendel gathered up his daughter, "time to get out of the house a little."

Taiba covered Shurka with a wool scarf, asked Yaakov Mendel to look after the girl and waved goodbye to them until their horse and cart disappeared from view. The horses galloped along the road leading to Ostrow Lubelski. The day was clear and bright and Shurka thirstily drank in the landscape. She saw the farmers mending the fences which had broken during the winter's storms and the young calves running about the fields. As they neared the town she saw the great forest beyond the hills and the green fields.

"Papa, look, what's that after the fields?" She pulled at Yaakov Mendel's sleeve and pointed towards the forest, where the tops of the tall pine trees were tangled together and the old oak trees stood thick and solid.

"Where?"

"Over there, far, far that way... what? You don't see? There, look Papa!" She did not understand why he did not see the straight white treetops that moved freely in the wind. "Papa, look, there, the trees are dancing. Look how pretty!"

"I don't see anything pretty about the forest."

"What is it called?"

"Parczew Forest. Remember, it is a bad place."

"Please, Papa, take me there," Shurka pleaded but her father signaled to her not to speak, and told her that it was impossible. The Parczew Forest was dangerous, not good for people - there were swamps and big mosquitos and small children must not go in there.

"Remember what I said - never go into the forest!" His voice was serious as he urged the horses onward.

The next morning, Shurka told Taiba about their trip. "Mama,

I saw the big forest of Parczew. Please, take me to the forest."

A cloud passed over Taiba's face. "No. It is forbidden to enter that forest."

"Why?" insisted the little Shurka, "Why is it forbidden to visit there?"

"Because the Parczew Forest is like a dark maze and those who do not know it could make a wrong turn and never find their way out. And those who do not know the paths well might slip and fall into the swamps."

"Are there also wolves and evil witches?

"Witches are only in fairy tales. Enough, my girl."

"And wolves?"

"I don't know."

Shurka stood on the tips of her toes hoping she might manage to see the wolves and witches in the great forest.

"You know Ivan, the son of Marisha the laundress, told me that sometimes when his mother is busy, he takes the horse and travels far far away, up to the forest."

"Alone in the great forest?" Taiba marveled. "But the great forest is very far from here."

"Yes that is what he says. And once Ivan even brought me a sweet fruit called a blueberry that he picked there. He said that in the great forest there are golden lizards and birds with diamonds on their heads."

"Ivan is stupid. He does not know what he is talking about."

"Can I go with him, just once? He promised to look after me. Please Mama." The mysterious forest stirred up her wildest imagination.

"Absolutely not," Taiba put her foot down. "Little girls do not go to the forest." And Taiba, seeing Shurka's face crumple, hugged her. "Enough. Better you should help me roll out the dough. We will make apple cake together."

But Shurka was fascinated by the fairy tales of the great forest.

"Ivan's grandfather told him that the king of the forest goes around there and he is evil. He breaks the trees and searches for the souls of small children."

"I've heard enough," Taiba scolded her. "The king of the forest is a myth that people invented. Now help me with the dough."

But Shurka was stubborn.

"He said that the king of the forest looks for babies and then he takes their souls. And if he can't find babies he catches children and after that the grownups. Is it really so Mama? Will he catch me?" She burst into tears.

Taiba, like all the villagers, had heard the myths of the king of the forest. She sat little Shurka on her lap and comforted her.

"Don't listen to Ivan. He is only trying to frighten you. Fairy tales do not really happen. Don't worry, my little princess, your father and I will always take care of you. We won't let anyone hurt you - certainly not the king of the forest." Taiba pulled little Shurka in close, as though trying to protect her, and Shurka hugged her doll Alinka and promised to protect her from the bad wolves.

"Just do not go alone to the forest... promise me."

"Never, never, never," Shurka promised. She understood; it was dangerous there. Bad wolves wandered around in the forest.

So she learned to fear the Parczew Forest. How could she have known that just a few years later it would be that very forest that would save and protect her from the wolves that gathered in the west?

Polish Jewry between the Two World Wars

When Poland gained independence, in the years 1918-1920, riots against Jews began in hundreds of cities and towns.

Jews made up as much as 30% or more of the population of Poland's main cities. In the year 1931, there were 3,131,900 Jews in Poland (including Danzig). It seems that during the eight years prior to the outbreak of the World War II, their number rose to 3,300,000, the largest diaspora population at that time.

The national movement in Poland already regarded the Jews as an alien and even disturbing element. While the Polish in-telligentsia and liberal circles tended to call for the inclusion of Jews in society, in reality, most of the Jewish population con-tinued to live separately in insular communities and separate neighborhoods, and were treated with hostility by their Polish neighbors.

During the second half of the '30s, antisemitism in Poland reached a new peak. The general population widely supported the idea of denying Jews the right to reside in Poland or at least in part of the country. The Jews of Poland underwent a harsh process of impoverishment. This humiliation reflected the fracture and the general poverty of the country.

In the areas of education, culture and communal and political activity, the Jews enjoyed a great deal of freedom, and sometimes even received encouragement and support from the state. Poland's Jewry became the epicenter of global Jewry in terms of national, political, social and cultural activity. At that time the Polish Jews, despite their declining economic status, adhered to the values of tradition - and were thus particularly devoted to ideological and national fields of activity. This included the establishment of Jewish theaters, newspapers, literary salons and many cultural activities, primarily independent initiatives to protect Jewish existence in Poland and a vigorous Zionist organization with the aspiration, particularly among youth groups, of immigration to the Land of Israel.

2.

And the spring returned again to Marianowka, and again the sun rose and Shurka could go out to the yard. They planted new bulbs in the marigold and chrysanthemum beds. And just as Mama had promised, Shurka's beloved storks returned to their home at the top of the pole and set about restoring the old nest. Shurka was happy to see them and every morning she and Taiba would put fresh water and seeds out underneath the pole. Her mother told her that the storks would now be busy hatching their eggs and raising the tiny chicks.

One day when Shurka was four, Mama told her that she, like the storks, was waiting for her own little chick.

"But people don't have chicks."

"Very true!" laughed Taiba, "The human chick is a baby. And very soon we will have a baby and you will have a brother or maybe a sister."

"I want a sister," said Shurka. "We can play together with my dolls."

Shurka was four when her sister Devorah was born. Three years later, another daughter joined the family. When Mama was heavy and supported her back with both hands, Shurka knew that a new baby was on its way and that the sweet baby smell would again fill the small house and that Mama would be even busier... and that she would have new roles to fill.

"You are my eldest," Mama would say, embracing Shurka. "I

depend on you." Shurka's brother, Shlomo, was born a few years later, when she was ten years old and a student in elementary school.

And again the spring came and the little garden that surrounded the house bloomed in yellow, purple, and red.

The scent of the lilac bush perfumed the air. The chickens resumed roaming the yard, and Mama allowed Shurka to go out and play with the neighboring children. They ran around the big field in front of the house, making goalposts from rocks and kicking a big rag ball through them. They ran and raced each other, played hide-and-seek and catch or strolled for pleasure and gathered flowers from the field.

Little Shimon, who everyone called "Shim'leh," was among Shurka's companions. He was the son of Menachem Leib and Leah Zursky, the good neighbors who lived in the house across the way. Little Shim'leh would run around with the children, throwing the ball and occasionally glancing at Shurka.

"She loves me, she loves me not," he would mumble as he pulled petals off the flowers. Once he gathered his courage and followed her home, where he straightened up to his full height and in a serious voice declared, "When we grow up, I want you to be my wife."

Shurka was stunned and began to cry and Shim'leh handed her a white handkerchief and said, "Please don't cry - I want to marry you, only you. What do you say?" And Shurka? She blushed and escaped into the house.

"That's what he said?" Her mother laughed when Shurka told her what the neighbor's son had asked.

"Just like that. Marriage... it's like you and Papa?"

"Exactly."

"So I will marry Shim'leh."

"Listen," said Mama, "there is no rush to decide. You will have plenty of suitors ahead of you. You just have to choose the one that is best for you."

And Shurka imagined that, like Mama, she too would have a family, and she too would pour cold lemonade for passing merchants, and in the spring she would pick the ripe pears from the tree that would grow in her garden.

She did not yet know that the contract with Satan had already been signed and that fate was about to change its course. Shim'leh, her first admirer, would lose his father and his brothers one morning when the evil messengers came to do the devil's bidding. She also could not have known that the family she would build for herself would have to flee far from that pear tree, far from the window she loved, and that they would be forced to hide in the great forest that Ivan, the son of the laundress had told her about.

During the Passover holiday, the family would go to visit Taiba's parents, Saba Shmuel and Grandma Hanna. They lived in the nearby town of Ostrow Lubelski, not far from the glass factory that Taiba's father ran. It was the biggest city that Shurka had ever seen.

In preparation for the trip, Taiba would make oat and butter cookies, fill jars with pear jam, and make bundles of blankets and holiday clothes. Papa Yaakov Mendel would harness the gray horse to the wagon loaded with the four children, cover them well with the blankets, whistle to the horse, and they would set off.

Shurka loved visiting her grandparents. She loved the sweet cooking smells that filled up the big house and her grandfather's big bed with soft cushions scattered over it that she could disappear into. And Grandma, who always had special sweets for her, would tell her stories of princesses and knights before she went to sleep. But there was something else. Shurka knew that Grandma Hanna always saved remnants of fabric for her - soft cotton and colorful silks, and other enticing bits of cloth she had set aside from her extensive inventory. Grandma Hanna was a seasoned merchant who had a hand in various businesses. Selling fabric was one of them.

"Here, take these and ask your mother to sew you a new skirt, or a dress for your beloved Alinka doll." Later Grandma told Taiba that a girl should have a profession and suggested that as Shurka grew up, she should learn to sew.

"Being a seamstress is a good profession."

"She still has time, why must she decide now?"

"The child loves fabric, and likes to watch me sew, and don't forget that it can be very lucrative work. These days a girl needs a profession, not like you with your rough hands from all that village labor," said Grandma and Taiba knew that her mother did not like the idea of a good-looking young woman such as herself doing farm work.

"I love what I do. We have a successful farm, all from our own hard work," Taiba protested and Grandma Hanna nodded her head.

On the evenings preceding the holidays or on Fridays, neighbors and friends from the village and from nearby villages would gather at Saba Shmuel's house, and pray in the big room that served as the village synagogue. The women in the adjoining room would listen to the men's voices praying; they would chat quietly or join them in song and prayer. Shurka loved to join in too. She would peer at the worshipers from between the wooden slits and note their closed eyes and would marvel at their swaying from side to side, wrapped in a white cloth that Papa called a "*tallit*."

On Simchat Torah the family would go to celebrate in the town of Ostrow Lubelski, where, as Papa explained to her, there was a big Jewish community.

"More Jews than in our village?"

"Many more," Papa explained, one-third of all the residents there are Jewish. More than fifteen hundred."

"And everyone has enough eggs?"

"Sure. Here they trade; they buy for cheap and sell for a profit."

"What do they sell?"

"Mostly clothes, shoes and fabric."

The Jewish community of Ostrow Lubelski was old and prosperous. In the synagogue with smooth walls and round windows, Shurka and Taiba would go up to the women's section where they could watch as the Rabbi very carefully, as if holding a newborn baby, would remove the Torah scroll covered in embroidered silk from the wooden cupboard. He kissed it lovingly, prayed, sang and danced with it. Afterwards he passed it along to other men. When Yaakov Mendel's turn came, Shurka ran after him and held onto his coat, proud of her father. And after that Papa would pass the Torah along to someone else, lift Shurka onto his shoulders and dance. Sometimes the Poles would come to watch the Jews celebrate, bringing along good wine to share and enthusiastically applauding the singing and dancing.

Alas, today, in the place where the temple once stood, there is a not-so-special, regular house and the once-beautiful synagogue has been turned into a derelict storage space for clothing. There is not a trace left in the town of the glorious days of the building. The Star of David painted on it is gone and so too is the seven-armed menorah which stood in the large entrance. The Torah scroll wrapped in silk has long since gone to ashes.

And life continued on as usual.

As though nothing could happen.

On Rosh Hashana, the Jewish New Year, Shurka would receive new winter clothes. For Sukkot, the two Yaakov Mendel would build a sukkah, a temporary shade structure recalling the Israelites journey out of Egypt, from the trunks of elm trees that grew in the forest. They would stretch white sheets around the walls and Taiba would hang the paper decorations that she had made. For Hanukkah, Papa would make Shurka a menorah from wood that she would paint and decorate with golden stars. But of all the Jewish holidays, Shurka loved Passover the most. She would drink in the scent of spring blossoms; touch the soft leaves that sprouted on tree branches, and dance in the fields that the sun caressed after the long winter of snow. Most of all she loved the holiday meal held in the home of Saba and Grandma. The whole family would gather around the festive Seder table, dressed elegantly in their holiday attire. The silver candlesticks, specially polished in preparation for the holiday, decorated the table adorned with its white tablecloth and laid with the blue china dishes. To Shurka, everything seemed to be straight out of the magical world of a fairy tale.

Shurka's special task was to open the door for Elijah the prophet. She was sure that he visited their home and drank the sweet wine that they prepared for him. "Soon he will come to us with the Messiah, Ben David," they would sing and Shurka, whose eyes were already closing, after the wonderful meal and the long Seder service, would ask her parents not to forget to wake her when Elijah came, because she wanted to present him with the silver cup that Taiba and Yaakov Mendel usually kept in the wooden cupboard.

"We had it good," Shurka would tell her grandchildren, many years later. "How could anyone have known...? It was so good then, of the full life we had there, now all that remains is in our memory."

***

When Shurka turned six, like all the other village children, she went to the Polish school in the neighboring village. The school was a small stone structure surrounded by a flower garden.

Every morning the village children - Jews and Christians alike - would gather beside Shurka's home and call to her to come and walk to school with them. They were a small group of children, with schoolbags over their backs and they would sing and chase one another or compete over finding the roundest stone or being first to spot a green bird. The bigger children would lead the way and look out for the younger ones.

On winter days, Taiba would come to pick up Shurka from the school and put on her galoshes so that she could walk back in the snow.

"Tell me, little one, how was your day today?"

"It was good, Mama," Shurka embraced her mother around the neck.

"And when the teacher asked you questions, you knew the answers?"

"I gave the right answers and I got a gold star."

"What do you most love to learn about?"

"I love to hear about how things used to be, to learn about

the way people used to live." Shurka waved goodbye to her classmates. Taiba put on Shurka's coat and buttoned it up.

In fourth grade, Shurka was chosen to manage the class journal, and the job pleased her. "Out of all the children, they chose me," she told her father that evening, as she sat writing studiously in the journal. "The teacher said that I am responsible."

"And an attentive student," Taiba added proudly. "She always knows the answer to her teacher's questions." And Papa Yaakov Mendel gazed upon his daughter with pride.

3.

At the school in Wolka Zablocka, as in the other small villages nearby, the children studied until the age of 14. Only a few went on to the high school in the neighboring city.

Girls generally did not continue their studies and made do with eight years of schooling. But Shurka was among the very few girls lucky enough to be able to go on.

When Shurka turned 15 and was already a beautiful young woman, her family decided that the time had come for her to learn a profession. It was her mother's idea, and it pleased Shurka. But they had to overcome Yaakov Mendel's resistance; he did not understand why she needed a profession.

"She should stay here and help you."

"It would be good for her to know something else besides looking after chickens."

"Soon enough she will get married and then her husband will look after her."

Aunt Alinka also pursed her lips when she heard the idea.

"What for? She should stay at home and help," she said. "Taiba don't forget you have three other children that need looking after."

"I can manage, and Devorahleh helps me with everything."

"You didn't study," insisted Uncle Yaakov Mendel.

"A woman needs a skill," insisted Taiba.

"As my dear brother-in-law said, a daughter's place is with her family, until the day comes for her to get married and build her own home. Since when do girls need more than that?" The aunt argued and Yaakov Mendel said that in his day the girls didn't even learn to read...

"Times have changed, Yaakov Mendel," said Taiba, "a new wind is blowing. These days even pretty princesses such as ours need a profession."

In the end Yaakov Mendel gave in.

"I understand," he said as he ran his hand through his beard. "And what do you wish to learn, my child?"

Shurka immediately replied that she was thinking of learning to sew.

"Why sewing? What's wrong with managing a farm like Mama? I will teach you to look after sheep, to milk, to help the cows give birth."

"That does not interest me."

"And if one day we should move to the land of our forefathers..."

"Then I will be able to sew clothes for the pioneers."

"But why sewing in particular?"

"Because that is what I love to do."

"You also love to tell stories to your sister Ruska."

"It's always useful to know how to sew. If you want, I'll sew you a new coat," Shurka insisted, and Mama went over to the box of clothes and showed Papa the elaborate dresses that Shurka had sewn for her doll Alinka from the scraps of fabric that Grandma Hanna had given her. There were also lace-trimmed aprons, the pleated skirt she had made for her sister Devorah, and the scarf she had knit for her brother Shlomo.

"See for yourself, Yaakov Mendel, our girl is talented," said Mama and she pointed to the green holiday dress that Shurka had sewn for her. "And don't forget that after she finds a groom and is married - God willing - she can make clothes for our grandchildren."

Shurka blushed.

Yaakov Mendel smiled. The thought of the grandchildren he would one day bounce on his knees always filled him with joy and he gave his daughter a kiss.

It was decided that Shurka should learn her trade in the nearby city of Ostrow Lubelski where sewing and knitting were taught. The question was where she would live. Shurka asked to live in the home of her friend who was already studying there but her parents felt that a decent girl should not live alone but with her relatives. So she was sent to the house of her Aunt Mina, the eldest sister of Yaakov Mendel.

"My sister has a big house," Yaakov Mendel assured her when they had already left the village. "You'll be comfortable there."

They decided that Yaakov Mendel would bring his daughter to the city and take care of all the necessary arrangements.

On their way, they passed by a great forested area.

"See there? That's the Parczew Forest," Papa pointed at the big oak trees being blown about by the wind.

Shurka looked and replied, "I remember once when I was little and you took me out in the wagon with you and we saw the forest."

"That was a different side," Papa corrected her.

"But it was also big."

"You were small then so the forest next to the village looked big to you. The Parczew Forest is enormous - you could walk there for days and still not reach civilization."

"Ivan would always say that the ruler of the forest roams there and steals the souls of small children."

"Superstitions!" spat Papa scornfully. "Don't believe his nonsense. It is full of mosquitos and swamps. Only those who know the forest well can find their way through."

"You know, Papa?" Shurka chuckled, "I believed everything that Ivan told me and I was so scared. At night I would hide under my blanket so that the ruler of the forest wouldn't find me." The two of them laughed, remembering the curious child she was, who had so wanted to visit the great forest.

They drove for about an hour along the rough road, stopping several times to remove rocks or branches that had fallen in winter storms.

The aunt and uncle hurried out to greet them, "Is this little Shurka?" They laughed.

"This is Shurka the sewing student!" exclaimed Shurka.

Her relatives had an extra room available, and Shurka raced to her new room and was pleased to see that it was spacious and filled with light.

From the big window she could see the street, the pretty sidewalks dotted with street lamps, the large shop windows displaying dresses from fabrics she had never seen before in her life, the hawkers and vendors announcing their wares, the elegant carriages and the big city people.

"They are so different from the people in our village," she said to her aunt.

"We are city people, but this is a small city. Just wait until you get to Lublin."

It was agreed that Shurka would attend her studies five days a week, and spend the Sabbath with her family. The sewing school was close to her aunt's house. She could walk there and arrive in her classroom in five minutes. She learned how to operate a sewing machine and how to distinguish between different kinds of materials, the running stitch, the basting stitch and the slip stitch.

At first she was only allowed to sew scarves and tablecloths. Later she learned how to make patterns, to plan and design dresses and shirts.

"Tell me," Taiba would ask her when she came back home to the village, "how is everybody?"

And Shurka would tell of her progress in her studies, of the new friends she had made, about the city people and how they were always in a hurry, and of her cousins and many relatives.

"Are they kind to you?"

"Very much so, all of them. But I most love visiting Aunt Nehama and Uncle Yitzhak."

"I am happy to hear that," said Taiba. "My brother-in-law, Yitzhak, is really an excellent person. All of us were happy when my sister married him. And they have a big family - touch wood."

"They have seven wonderful children," Shurka's eyes sparkled. "I feel comfortable there."

For one whole year Shurka studied sewing and lived away from home, got a taste of city life and made new friends. At the end of the year, her studies ended and she returned to live with her family in the village.

In the mornings she would help her mother bake bread and make soup and in the afternoons she would go to her sewing table and mend her sisters' dresses and sew new clothes for her brother.

After dinner, when Shurka usually helped Taiba clear the table or sweep the floor, Yaakov Mendel would look at his daughter and saw that she had become a beautiful young woman.

"What do you say about this daughter of ours?"

"Soon the boys will start coming around."

"She's still young."

"Soon she will turn seventeen and she will be ready to begin her own life," interrupted Aunt Alinka, who always had something to say. "Even the matchmaker has started hinting that the time has come to find a suitable match for the princess."

"The heart works in mysterious ways," said Taiba. She could sense what was happening in her daughter's heart. Shurka's face reddened - whenever the topic arose, she would blush. She had not revealed to anyone that her heart was set on a particular young man.

His name was Avraham Orlitzky, the son of Ella and David, a trader of religious items. Though they had never said so much as a word to one another, she became lightheaded whenever she thought of him. Of all the young men around, Avraham Orlitzky was the most handsome. He was tall with strong hands and a piercing gaze, his lips fixed in a smile of perpetual amusement. Everybody liked him, Jews and Gentiles alike.

Shurka, though she was in fact considered to be one of the most beautiful and industrious young women in the region and was spoken of kindly in the nearby villages, worried that he had never even noticed her. She was, after all, a farmer's daughter, while he belonged to an established and respected merchant family, and was considered by everyone to be an excellent and desirable match.

When did they meet?

When did she manage to fall in love with him?

They met at the celebrations for Simchat Torah at the town's main synagogue, where the crowd of people praying danced around the Torah while the children waved paper flags. Shurka felt someone staring at her.

"What happened to you?" Taiba laughed, knowing exactly what was going on.

"I suddenly felt a kind of heat around my heart," Shurka told her mother.

She looked over at him and he smiled back at her unabashedly. At that moment, she felt the earth quaking beneath her and her heart beat furiously.

Shurka panicked and quickly hid behind her mother. After all, a girl must be modest and not send signals to boys.

And Avraham Orlitzky? He smiled at her, waved hello to Taiba, and went to join the circle of dancers.

That same night Shurka dreamed that she was walking into a sea of candles and before her stood the smiling Avraham. His handsome face was lit up.

"Did you see?" Taiba asked her Aunt Shifra, who lived in Lubartow, the following day.

"Of course," said the aunt, "everyone saw. What did you think?"

"She's still so young."

"It is clear that the girl needs to marry," said the aunt. "When you were her age you were already a mother. I met Mrs. Gottlieb the matchmaker today. She will come by to speak with you about the scholar's son who has come of age."

"Shurka won't want a matchmaker managing her life for her. Times have changed, I know her. My Shurka will marry whomever it is that she likes."

And Shurka listened, smiling. And at night she tossed and turned in her bed and dreamed of him.

They met again at the Hanukkah party which took place at Shurka's grandparents' home in Ostrow Lubelski. This time he looked over at her and smiled. Shurka smiled back at him and he approached her. They stood beside one another, embarrassed and dumbstruck.

Shurka hoped that no one would hear her heart beating. He was so close she could smell his breath. And while the others sang *Maoz Tzur* together, he leaned toward her and asked if he could come and visit her in her family home. Shurka nodded her head and said that the he would be welcome and Avraham asked her if she understood why he wanted to visit.

She understood very well. A flash of heat washed over her face and Shurka nodded her head, and said aloud that he would have to speak with her parents. Avraham smiled and ran his hand over her hair, and Shurka knew immediately. She had never felt so warm and so happy.

When she told her mother about it later, Taiba said, "my girl, that's love. My daughter is in love."

"It is written in the stars," said Yaakov Mendel, reddening. "Like our ancestors Avraham and Sara, I understood immediately that it is from above." And everyone laughed.

Later, Avraham and Shurka walked through the paths of the village and the neighbors looked at them and said what an attractive couple they were and asked Yaakov Mendel when they would finalize the contract already.

They were married in early summer. They held the wedding party on the Orlitzky family's big property. Long tables covered with white tablecloths were set up on the grass and were laid with the food prepared by friends: stews, fish patties, stuffed fish, chicken, and a three-tiered wedding cake made by the local baker.

Shurka wore the wedding dress that Taiba had kept for her in the big wooden chest. Shurka added blue embroidered flowers on the sleeves of the white silk dress, and wore her grandmother's pearl necklace. Everyone said she looked like a queen under the chuppah.

"To the beautiful bride," Yaakov Mendel raised his glass.

Taiba blushed and said, "Enough, touch wood." And all the guests laughed and clinked glasses with one another.

There were those who said: Look at that, the bride comes from a farmer's family, while Avraham Orlitzky deserves a bride from a rich and established family like his own. And there were others who said: Look how beautiful she is, she deserves a husband even richer than he is. And the other girls from the village and the city looked enviously upon the attractive couple.

"My beautiful bride," Avraham whispered to her, "I promise you that we will be happy. You will be my Queen Sarah." And Shurka held his hand and could feel the fluttering of the wings of happiness.

In the middle of the wedding party, when guests were already onto their third or fourth glass of wine, the orchestra was playing energetically, and boys and girls were dancing, a young couple entered the yard. They carried with them two large suitcases.

All at once, the music stopped and the dancing froze.

"Who are they?" guests asked one another.

"What are they doing here?"

'They came to a wedding in casual clothes?"

When the man of the house, Aharon Orlitzky, noticed the couple, he got up from his seat and hurried toward them. All of the merrymakers followed with interest. They spoke for a few minutes, then Orlitzky led them into the house. When he returned, his face was red.

"Who are they?"

"The children of Yosef, a friend from childhood. Yosef and his wife Miriam."

"And what brought them to us?"

"Not now, my dear, not now. Now let us celebrate."

The guests did not move. There was something disquieting in the couple that had disrupted the celebration.

Aharon raised his glass to the newlyweds and said, "Jews, today we celebrate."

And once more glasses were clinked together and the orchestra started to play.

Only later, toward evening, when the guests had dispersed and just a few family members remained to help clean up the yard, was it revealed that the couple who had shown up unannounced had escaped from Berlin because of the disturbing atmosphere created by Hitler, who had promised the Germans that he would cleanse their country of Jews.

"That man is dangerous," said the young man. "He doesn't even try to hide his hatred for us. He has already passed new laws, and each day we wake up to some new decree."

"And where...?"

"East. It's no good staying here. Listen, come with us."

"Berlin is far away," they told them. "And this Hitler is a passing phase."

"I refuse to worry," said Aharon Orlitzky, and his wife announced that she put her faith in her husband - he always knew.

The year was 1937.

Here they were cutting into a three-layer cake but somewhere to the west the sky was already darkening. A small man with the eyes of Satan was screaming in the squares, threatening the world, and blaming Taiba and Yaakov Mendel's people. But back in Eastern Poland, they still did not believe and did not want to know.

In the little village, Shurka and Avraham celebrated their

love, embracing one another and planning their future. Together they dreamed of the children that would be born to them and the grandchildren that would follow.

"What good fortune," said Shurka, placing her hand on her husband's. "Imagine if we had immigrated to Eretz Israel... How would we have met?"

"This is how destiny wanted it, Shurka," laughed Avraham. "And besides, there was no way we would not have met. We are made for each other."

And destiny?

Destiny has its own way of unfolding, dear reader. If the family had immigrated to Israel, our entire story would have ended differently.

4.

Avraham Orlitzky was proud of what he had. He brought his young bride to the charming, spacious wooden house that he had rented for them in the center of the little village of Glebokie, close by to Shurka's village. Their friends called her Avraham's Sarah.

With the money they received as wedding gifts, the young couple bought new furniture which filled the rooms of their home.

They had a sideboard of walnut wood, a broad dining table covered by a tablecloth embroidered by Taiba with blue lilies, a big bed, and a red carpet from Avraham's parents. In the flower garden out front there were ducks, rabbits and chickens, and even one rooster with an elaborate comb. Avraham called him Achashverosh.

"Why Achashverosh, of all the names?" laughed Shurka, and Avraham stroked the rooster.

"Because he changes girlfriends every other day and besides, take a look at his glorious crown."

Right beside the house stood a tall pole topped by a stork's nest that Shurka made sure to attend to, regularly bringing fresh water and crumbs. There was peace in their spacious home. Avraham was occupied with his business, going from village to village, buying and selling religious items, candlesticks and precious objects, while his young wife embroidered bedspreads, sewed curtains, prepared noodles and dumplings, and filled jars with jam she had prepared, just as she had learned from Taiba. Avraham painted the fence white and on a big wooden board wrote "Here live the lovers Avraham and Sarah."

"Why such a big sign?" asked Shurka.

Avraham tenderly ran his hand over the sign and said, "I hope that soon we will fill it up with more names." Shurka rested her head against his chest and smiled.

One morning the sound of wheels disturbed their routine. A large wagon entered the village. It stopped beside their house and from it descended Taiba and Yaakov Mendel, with smiles upon their faces. Shurka quickly went to greet her parents who pointed to the wagon. Inside stood her old Singer sewing machine. Shurka stroked its shiny wood and turned the wheel.

"I missed it so much," she whispered.

"We thought... that maybe soon you will need it, if you know what I mean." Taiba smiled and Shurka blushed.

And Yaakov Mendel said, "Hush, woman, don't you see that the child is embarrassed?"

5.

Avraham's business flourished. Every morning he would leave Glebokie and set out with his wagon filled with wares. On his return, having sold all of his merchandise, the horse galloped lightly and Avraham thanked God for his good fortune.

"Not just luck." Shurka blushed. "In the village they tell me that everyone wants to buy from you. Your merchandise is the best and you are an honest man who has never deceived anybody."

"I am happy to hear that. It is said that a good name is better than good oil."

"And you are a merchant with a good name - even the goyim say it about you."

"The most important thing is that I can sense what the clients want. Here, look what I brought you from the city."

Avraham would often give Shurka a new scarf or lace material for the tablecloths.

Shurka continued to decorate their nest. She hung the lace curtains that she had embroidered, sewed pillowcases and knit wool socks for her husband.

When the spring came and the trees wore green and the storks returned to their nests at the tops of Glebokie's poles, Shurka had something to tell her husband. That same evening, she set the table with a festive tablecloth and flowers she had picked from their small garden.

"What's the occasion?" Avraham asked and Shurka blushed.

"You're blushing," he said. "Is it serious? Maybe we should speak after I finish my work."

"No, wait," she stopped him. "I want to speak with you."

"What do you want to say, my dear?" he asked and his heart, predicting what was coming, beat furiously.

"You know what the storks do in the spring..." Shurka looked at the floor.

"The storks? I don't understand," said Avraham, who knew his wife and understood that Shurka was not really referring to the storks. "What do the storks do, my beloved Sarah?"

"They brood and then—"

"And then?" interrupted Avraham.

"They enlarge the family," Shurka finished the sentence and turned to peer out the window. She was too embarrassed to look her husband in the eye.

"Wait," Avraham pulled his young wife into his lap, "what are you telling me?"

"That our nest will also receive a new addition."

"My beautiful queen... my Shurka," he mumbled excitedly and led his wife gently, as though she were some precious and delicate instrument, to the chair.

"And when is the happy day?" he asked and with a red face, Shurka indicated with her fingers that she was already in the second month.

"In seven months I will be a father... a father... Papa Avraham, Papa and Mama..." Avraham stood up on his feet and kissed Shurka lovingly, then hurried to his parents' house which was not far, to tell them the good news.

The house filled up with relatives and friends who immediately gave them various bits of strange advice and piled up foods suitable for a woman in pregnancy. By the next day, all of the residents of the nearby villages knew that Shurka and Avraham were expecting a child.

And when Shurka passed on her way to the market or to visit friends, villagers - Christians and Jews alike - would invite her to their home, offer her a place to sit or a glass of fresh lemonade. Sarah and Avraham were beloved by everyone.

Now Shurka was occupied, not just looking after their small plot of land, but also by preparing for the baby that would be born when the time came "with God's help," as everyone said. She whitewashed and painted, and at nights she sewed tiny clothes. The wheel of her sewing machine spun furiously and she embroidered little blue forget-me-nots on bolts of soft cotton.

Mama Taiba came to help, and the two of them would take out the tiny articles of clothing and stroke them lovingly.

"I hope it will be a girl," Shurka would say to Avraham when they strolled through the village in the evenings.

And Avraham would support his wife affectionately and whisper to her that whatever may come will be welcome.

"And you know what they say: a daughter is a sign of sons."

In the last month of Shurka's pregnancy, Taiba moved to Glebokie to live in the house of the young couple. She wanted to be with her daughter when the time came, to assist her, and to help deliver her first grandchild. The two women were busy with preparations for the baby that would soon be born. Avraham built a wooden cradle and painted it white and Yaakov Mendel hung a lamp from the ceiling of the room.

One night at the end of January, as a snowstorm raged outside, Shurka woke Avraham, her face blanched with pain. "I think—"

"What?" shouted Avraham.

"—that the labor pains have begun," she said.

And he, bright with excitement and happiness, woke Taiba to look after his wife, harnessed the wagon and hurried to the neighboring village to bring the midwife.

"You never saw a happier man when he held his little daughter," the midwife later told the villagers. "His eyes sparkled like diamonds."

He placed the baby on her mother's belly and whispered his love to her and she smiled as though she understood her father's words.

"Let's call her Irena," suggested Shurka. "After my grandmother Irena who once lived with us. She taught me to roll out dough and to sing songs about the wind and rain."

Avraham nodded his head in agreement, "Excellent. We will call her Irena, which means peace." And a smile lit up the baby's face, as though she understood, and Avraham hugged the two of them.

The three of them had become a family: Papa, Mama and little Irena with skin the color of honey and eyes that sparkled. Irena loved to fall asleep on her father's belly while Shurka sang softly to her as she folded the cloth diapers which smelled of talcum powder. It seemed that the world in which Irena gurgled happily was a good and benevolent one.

And happiness kept on blossoming. But while her parents were still marveling at Irena's beautiful skin and her blue eyes and blessing their good fortune, somewhere, generals with swastikas on their lapels began to plan the first steps of the war. The factories put their employees to work making cannons and rifles, and the big production plants made tanks, while engineers designed planes to carry deadly bombs. A mob applauded the small man who screamed and blamed the Jews for all of Germany's troubles; while in the little village Avraham and Sarah danced with their daughter. Welcome to the year 1938. A new baby had come into the world.

Elsewhere too, the first steps were taken toward the great destruction. Between November 1 and 9, 1938, a pogrom against the Jews took place all across the Third Reich. The Great Synagogue in Berlin, a magnificent and historic building was destroyed. "Kristallnacht" was called such because of the shards of glass that scattered everywhere that night after the destruction sown by Hitler's henchmen.

That same month, November 1938, far from the shouts of Berlin's great but battered Jewish community, Shurka and Avraham continued their daily life. Sometimes Avraham would return home looking pale, bringing stories of Jews who were fleeing east from terrible new laws enforced by that screaming mustache or because of the expulsion of Jews from universities. Yet still they were steeped in their own happiness, telling one another that clouds always lift eventually and that that mad clown was merely threatening.

Avraham and Shurka gazed upon Irena. She turned ten months old and could sit and walk while holding onto her parents hands, and gurgle several words.

September of 1939 came and Irena was twenty months old. She was a lively and smiling child, beloved by all. She would run about the yard, chasing after the white chickens on her short legs and picking flowers to give to her mother. She would help her father gather eggs from the chicken house. "This is Irena, my princess," Avraham would introduce her to everyone, adding with a smile, "But of course! Her mother is Queen Shurka."

Irena loved her doll Alinka, that her mother had made for her. Saba Yaakov Mendel brought her a yellow chick that ran around the yard and Grandma Taiba knitted her a wool hat for winter days and told her about the storks. All of her aunts and uncles admired their little niece and would carry her on their shoulders and run around with her in the fields.

Avraham and Shurka dreamed of expanding their family. They wanted many children to fill their house with their little voices, laughter and songs. Avraham was certain their happiness would only grow.

But at that same time - while Irena was pulling on Achashverosh's tail and playing with her doll Alinka - the Germans invaded Poland. Hitler, the unstoppable Satan, continued his military push to the east. This time it was impossible to ignore. Poland surrendered almost without a fight. In the face of the powerful Germans, the Polish defense system collapsed like a house of cards.

Frightening reports arrived in the little villages in the district of Lublin. But so far the Germans were no more than rumors. Only stories. Nobody had seen so much as one German soldier yet. Everyone tried to continue as usual.

Avraham and Shurka learned of the goings-on from the merchants who moved among the villages and sometimes brought news. But they, like everyone else, did not give in to worry, even when the warning signs became more obvious and more frequent.

"You have nothing to fear," said their Gentile neighbors, when they told on another the troubling news. "You've been here more or less since we've been here, more than two hundred years. Who would tell you to leave?"

The news got worse from one day to the next. There were rumors of murder and robbery and of arrests and harassment. But in the villages, the main thing people worried about was whether the rain would come on time.

"They occupied Poland, so what?" Poles said to one another. The Jews nodded their heads.

So what?

So Poland had already been conquered by the Germans once before.

So what?

We went through that war, we went through riots, there were hard times, we will get through this too.

Hitler continued to speak and shout in the public squares. He threatened and threatened and did not hide his opinion about what he called "the Jewish Problem." He saw Jews as defiling the land of Europe, as Europe's enemies. In Germany they had already begun to kick Jewish lecturers out of the universities, Jews were robbed with no legal recourse, and many were arrested on charges of treason. Many restrictions were placed on them, limiting their movements and their lives.

"He won't dare touch us," Jews said to one another when they gathered to pray on Shabbat. "He will shout and shout and eventually calm down and the world will return to the way it was." Several months later, Polish Jews were ordered to wear the yellow patch.

The village was still quiet and serene and in Sarah's belly a new human chick was growing. Shurka knit a red woolen coat and a white scarf for Irena to keep her warm in the coming winter and fastened the yellow badge to her husband's shirt.

"Why me?" he asked, trying to defer wearing the badge, but she insisted. He traveled around a great deal and God forbid he should be caught without one. They had already heard of Jews who had been caught at the train station and had not been heard from since, of a woman who had lost her patch and had been beaten to death.

"You must do what they say."

"What is this?" asked Irena, and pointed to the yellow patch on her father's shirt.

"It's nothing," he reassured her and hinted to Shurka not to worry the little girl. "It's a kind of decoration."

"It's a Star of David. It's just like at the synagogue." Irena pointed at the patch and Avraham hugged her head and told her she really was a very smart little girl.

Shurka sighed. She did not tell her husband that she had recently been having recurring nightmares of the Parczew Forest: the swamps, the wolves looking for her, her Avraham lost in the woods...

One of the Jewish families that lived in Glebokie decided to take action. They secretly sold their house and traveled to Odessa, the port city, from where they planned to set off to Israel.

Before they left they came to bid farewell to Avraham and Sarah.

"What's the rush?"

"We must leave. We have to get far away from here."

"But I heard it said that it is hard in the land of our fathers. There are illnesses, swamps, and hardly any work," said Avraham. Shurka looked at her husband and thought that maybe it was time for them too to leave, to go there. At night she told her husband her fears.

"You needn't trouble yourself with such worrying," Avraham

stroked her belly. "Soon there will be a baby. Then we can see."

"I feel..."

"We won't move you while you are pregnant," he paused. "It's just a few more months, nothing will change."

"I heard that people are fleeing to the east, to Russia," Yaakov Mendel said when he came to visit the young couple.

"Russia is not an option," said Avraham. "I don't trust the Russians. They will hand over any escaped Jew to the Germans."

"But you trust the Germans?"

"The Germans are a cultured people."

"Have you heard what Hitler says?"

"He is a crazy clown, I believe with all my heart that our Polish friends will look after us. After all, we are one people, their language is our language and their culture is our culture." Avraham repeated his usual arguments. He saw no reason to worry.

"Hitler is the devil."

"But we have God."

"You are naive," said Yaakov Mendel. "They will be the first to turn us in. We have to start to think how to protect ourselves."

"You all worry too much. Wait and see - this Hitler will pass and we will be fine."

Mann Tracht, un Gott Lacht
Man Plans and God Laughs.

History has its own ways of managing men's paths through life while they are certain that it is all a matter of free will and decisions. Humanity believes that their fate is in their hands and then reality comes along and shows them otherwise.

The year was 1939.

The world was still in a deep slumber, just like Sleeping Beauty, cursed by the evil witch. None of the leaders was looking ahead; they did not want to recognize the signs of terror that had begun to form a crack in the world.

Meanwhile in their pretty house, Shurka and Avraham continued to build their future, to expand their home and their family.

Shurka and Avraham knew that the Lublin region, where their village was located, had now been completely conquered by the Germans. They heard the thunder of airplanes and the echoes of explosions. They watched the defeated Polish soldiers as they marched east toward the Russian border and the German soldiers in their boots marching victoriously as conquerors in their villages. They saw the lines of tanks that passed not far from their home, their trail clear on the ground. They knew that the mayor of their Polish village had been forced to cooperate with the invaders and had turned his offices over to them. They saw his drunken son, the idler, sitting in his place and surrendering to everything the Germans demanded.

They understood that Poland had lost its independence and that they were subject to German rule. Nonetheless, they remained compliant. They were not afraid.

The war would not touch them, or so they believed. It was happening somewhere else, at the front. And it would be over soon and life would return to its regular course. Besides, Poland had already known many long years of occupation.

"After all, politics," said Yaakov Mendel when he and Taiba had come to visit their beloved granddaughter, "is not for peaceable village people. Think about it, why should they bring the war to our area? What would be the point? It is a quiet and calm agricultural region whose people live off the fruits of their labor."

But the news kept coming in. Sometimes Jewish refugees who had escaped occupied Warsaw would stop at their house and tell them what was happening there.

"Why did you run away?" Sarah asked.

"We had to leave while we still could."

"What is so awful there?"

And they told her that the whole Jewish community of Warsaw was crammed inside a ghetto, and that food was scarce, many people were ill and there was no medicine. And not just that... now they were bringing Jews from the surrounding villages to the ghetto too and the crowding was terrible. The situation was bad and spreading throughout the streets. Shurka put out clean sheets and let the refugees rest in her home and looked far off into the distance, where the king of the forest searched for the souls of young children. Sometimes a timber trader would come with a newspaper that came from Lublin or Lubartow, but most of the information came from their friend the "Paritz" Luboskowitz.

Avraham was a well-connected merchant and occasionally undertook joint ventures with Paritz Luboskowitz and his family. Friendship and mutual trust grew between them. Paritz was often a guest in the home of Shurka and Avraham, and marveled at the stuffed fish or the almond cookies he was served. At other times he invited them to his big house, a two-hour drive from theirs, beside the city of Ostrow Lubelski.

The Paritz's house had a radio. Radios were scarce in those days, especially in small villages. It was from the radio that Paritz Andrey Luboskowitz learned what was happening to the west.

"Be careful," their Polish friend said once or twice, "I heard today that there will be more decrees on your brothers."

"You will look after us," laughed Avraham and the Paritz nodded his head, but his heart was heavy.

"I worry for you and for all the Jews with us."

That is how they discovered that Jewish businesses were being marked and confiscated, that Jews' freedom of movement was now limited and that Jews were prohibited from continuing to maintain educational and cultural systems or from holding public prayers. Professors were thrown out of the universities and there were stories of Gentiles shooting Jews and looting and robbing without any consequences.

"We will withstand it," Avraham would say to pacify his Polish friend.

"Are you sure?"

"Because if we look at history, we will see that the Germans never harmed the Jews when they occupied Poland in the First World War."

Meanwhile, Sarah's second pregnancy was already showing and Irena was telling stories to her Alinka doll. Rumors flourished and spread rapidly through the villages. The fabric trader told anybody who wished to listen what he had heard from the housewares merchant, who had heard from the egg seller, who had heard from the scholar...

And in time the rumors became reality.

And the flow of refugees grew.

Germany was no longer safe, nor was Poland, and many were packing up their belongings, selling what they could and moving east, toward the Russian border.

"You aren't worried about what could happen to you?" Shurka was asked by one of the refugees who had stopped to rest in her home with his family. She brought them hot soup and fresh bread.

"Poland is our homeland - why should we worry?"

"Didn't you hear what Hitler says about the Jews? He calls us the disaster of Europe. Didn't you hear about the murders, the looting, the abuse of our community?"

"This here is Poland," Shurka would answer them. "Jews, Christians - all of us are Polish. All of us are faithful citizens. The Polish will know to protect themselves and us."

Nobody thought then that the man who ranted at every square in Berlin had only taken his first step on his way to destroying the world.

One of the many victims of Kristallnacht was Otto Schneider, a history professor. After being let go from his position, and having his handsome house in the center of town confiscated, he and his family fled east and wanted to settle in Glebokie. He turned to Avraham for help in finding a house and work.

Avraham and Shurka willingly adopted the family, let them stay in their home and helped them to find a house not far away. On their small plot of land Avraham and Otto planted potatoes and onions.

But the father of the family found it hard to be happy in this faraway village. He missed his city in Germany, and its opera and concert halls. His delicate hands, the hands of an academic, were not suited to working the land. Avraham encouraged him to remain optimistic:

"It's temporary. Wait a year, maybe two and you can return to your culture in Berlin."

But the winter was harsh and the prices of wood rose. The German army confiscated property, cows and horses, and the dark clouds did not pass.

"Did you hear what the mad clown said in Berlin? Now he

is talking about a final solution to the Jewish problem," Otto said one evening when they sat in Avraham and Shurka's house sipping hot tea.

"The Germans are a cultured people," Avraham repeated his opinion. "They know that the Jews are important to the Polish economy. He will go on yelling and we will go on existing, just like Haman in his time. Relief and rescue will come."

"How?" said Otto, astounded. "Hitler isn't hiding his plans. And the Gestapo he established, those thugs in black feed on their hatred of the Jews. I am worried - some of my family is still there. They refused to leave." Shurka and Avraham looked awkwardly at him.

"And you, you aren't worried about what will happen?" Otto asked.

"Poland is not Germany," declared Avraham. "The Poles are our brothers - we are united in this."

While Avraham and Shurka nested in their home, sowing sunflower seeds in the summer and collecting the chestnuts in the winter, somewhere, beyond the mountains and the forests, the great monster, War, raised its evil head.

6.

The months passed and the situation got worse. Jews were fired from jobs with no explanation, their belongings taken away, valuables confiscated and their businesses handed over to Germans or Poles. It was forbidden for Jews to possess more than two thousand zloty in cash, and their bank accounts were frozen.

One evening, Paritz summoned Avraham to him.

"Look out," he said, "there is talk."

"What did you hear?"

"Not far from here they've been saying that today all the Jews from the towns and villages in western Poland that have already been occupied by Germany will be gathered together and transported by train to be contained in the big cities."

"Do you understand why?"

"The Germans are trying to replace the population in the occupied regions. The people being taken by trains have been forced from their homes."

"The Germans aren't stupid," said Avraham. "They have their own economic interests in mind - Jewish merchants like me, who the army needs to provide its supplies, won't be sent to the ghettos, for now."

"But everything is only 'for now.' They won't need you, you should leave or... I wouldn't take the risk."

"We can't travel now. Sarah's having a difficult pregnancy."

So Avraham stayed home for the time being. Then he had

to abandon his business. He was required to provide goods and products to the army units whose base was in Lublin and he could barely support his family. But he was a strong and optimistic man and he was sure that thanks to his good connections he would get through these hard times. Besides, in the large iron chest which he had recently buried in the yard, he kept gold coins, jewelry, silver objects and other valuables.

"Our insurance plan for a rainy day," Avraham would say to Shurka, who laughed when she saw him burying another coin in his treasury. "These days, who knows what will happen!" He stroked the chest and continued, "We should be prepared. Those who want to live will prepare for the worst."

Shurka shrugged. This fretting was familiar to her. Jews always worried: they were always suspicious that there was a coming storm even when the sun was shining. It did not occur to her that, thanks to the pearl earrings her parents had given her as an engagement present, the gold bracelets she had inherited from her mother, and the silverware and candlesticks they had received from Avraham's parents, they would be able to go on living.

The situation in their village and in the villages nearby steadily deteriorated. Now Avraham returned from his business in Ostrow Lubelski and Parczew, bringing more bad news.

He told them of the cities that had been occupied and the Jewish houses that had been looted, the confiscations and the expulsions. On the Paritz's radio Hitler declared that the Jews were a despicable and inferior race, an affliction that must be done away with. Sons of death that must be eliminated.

"Hunters told me that in the forest near the city of Ciechanow, the Germans gathered the Jews together and shot them."

And the same was happening outside this city and that city.

Little by little it became clear that they were sitting on a volcano ready to erupt.

"I am not being compliant," Avraham pacified the Paritz. "After the birth we will take action."

Shurka complained that it was hard to get food, that the vegetable stalls had emptied, that the farmers had raised the prices and that people were afraid.

"The way to fight the rumors is to ignore them," said Avraham, but Shurka insisted.

"You don't understand."

"The situation is temporary," Avraham calmed his worried wife. "War, a little discomfort, a few months... and everything will return to normal. Poland has seen days like these before. Why worry, Mamaleh? Our destiny is united with that of our neighbors, the Poles." He lovingly stroked Shurka's belly.

Then the rumors grew increasingly stubborn, bitter, and terrifying.

It was said that the capital, Warsaw, was being controlled by the Gestapo, a special army established by Hitler. It was said that they were kicking Jews out of their homes, the Poles were turning in their Jewish neighbors and looting their houses, that there was not enough food in the ghetto and people were dying of hunger, diseases were breaking out, and that the situation was only getting worse.

"Avraham, what will happen if they get here? Will they move us to the ghetto?" Shurka worried. Avraham tried to calm her. After all, the baby should be born very soon, and the sounds of war had not yet reached them. But Shurka was afraid. Her heart tightened with fear.

"What will happen if they come here too?" she asked.

"And why should they come?" said Avraham. "We are a little village somewhere in Poland - we do not interest anybody."

On one of the occasions when Avraham returned from his journeys, he told the others that in Parczew, they had confiscated the great town hall and established a German headquarters there.

The Jews said that at night they heard the heavy, stiff leather boots on the stones of the paths and the rattle of car motors driving quickly through the villages, but they still hoped that the war and the occupation were only temporary. Avraham did not tell his wife that his security chest was growing very heavy, that he hoarded every cent and prepared for the worst. He did not want to disturb her so close to the birth. But he was well aware that their time was running out.

7.

Those were hard times.

Unbearable for everyone.

The Germans emptied the conquered nation, confiscated property for the army's benefit, and began to clear out territories in the west of the country as part of the settlement plan.

The fate of the Jews in the Lublin area was no different than that of their brothers all over Poland. Their blood was worthless. Jews were required to wear a yellow badge, men between ages 14-65 were made to work forced labor - toiling in military camps, paving roads, carrying heavy loads - during which they were humiliated, beaten, and sometimes murdered. Some of them never returned and their fate remained unknown.

Jews were shot in the street without question, men's beards were brutally shorn in public, they were beaten or forced to clean the streets and to work any despicable job. Jews were required to mark their stores and to register their property.

Jews were forbidden to possess radio devices, and a curfew was imposed from evening until dawn. All of their rights were taken away, and their businesses were confiscated. And so there would be no confusion, the Germans declared that the Nuremberg Laws also applied to the Jews of Poland. The Poles, for the most part, cooperated with the forces of evil; they handed Jews over to the Germans and looted their belongings. But the worst still awaited them.

Winter of 1940 was coming and it was already hard to obtain fresh eggs and firewood. Shurka walked between the neighbors' houses, trying to exchange her hen eggs for flour, so she could make bread for her family.

"What will become of us? I can scarcely get a hold of flour or oil and the farmers are selling milk for exorbitant prices - how are we going to feed two babies?" Shurka despaired.

"Don't worry, you will take care of Irena and, when the time comes, also the baby soon to be born. Let me manage the war." Avraham was quick to pacify his wife and did not reveal that he was tossing and turning every night, unable to sleep. Shurka looked at him hopefully.

"Everything will be okay," Avraham continued. "We have friends, we have money, we have property. Let me worry about everything; you relax, my dear."

"How?"

"Trust me."

"They are saying that some small children were taken off the wagon on the main road to Ostrow Lubelski. They cut their sidelocks and beat the father."

"Enough, you must look at the whole picture. The Germans need us; they themselves said they must consider German economic interests."

"You believe them?"

"They won't touch the merchants whose job is to supply the army. We are safe. And your parents - the Germans need the agricultural produce that they are able to provide. Be strong, Shurka. Remember, we are a tough people, we will fight back."

News fragments gathered like dark clouds before a great storm. Shurka saw that many families had begun to abandon the village on their way east and the markets that were always bustling were practically empty. Agricultural produce was confiscated for the war effort, the horses and cattle were taken away and the strong men were ordered to go to labor camps in western Poland.

One night Paritz Luboskowitz came to their house. He was worried. The news that had gotten to him about cramming Jews into ghettos was decidedly ominous. He came to plead with Avraham and Shurka to save their own lives, to hurry, pack everything and go east, toward the Russian border, where many Jews had escaped.

"It's no longer a matter of debate; you must get out of here."

"How can we?" said Avraham stubbornly. "Soon the baby will be born - we can't set off on a long journey now. Maybe in a few months."

"Get started before the snow covers the roads."

"You are blowing it out of proportion my good friend," said Avraham, "I don't think the Germans are interested in our little village. It's not Warsaw or Lodz - there are only a few hundred Jewish families in this whole region - they don't even know we're here."

"Don't count on that. They will get here too. Hitler promised to erase the Jewish people - get going! If you need, I will lend you my horse."

Avraham listened thoughtfully and looked to Shurka. She stroked her belly lovingly.

Her head clouded with worry, and she asked, "What will become of my parents? My father won't abandon his plot or their family. We should wait... maybe the war will skip over us."

"You're a stubborn lot, you Jews," their friend Paritz Luboskowitz shook his head, "but this time your stubbornness won't pay off. Everyone knows the madman is doing more than just talking."

Avraham poured him a glass of cherry wine that he had hidden in the basement.

"We are Polish Jews - this is our language, our culture, our homeland."

"Just don't miss the train." Luboskowitz sighed at Avraham's obstinacy. "One thing I promise you is that my house will always be open to you, my friends. Your grandfather was a friend of my grandfather, I still remember the tunes he would sing to me and the stories he would tell."

In the spring of 1941, a letter arrived at Avraham and Shurka's house. "What happened?" Shurka asked her husband.

"Everything is alright," he tried to soothe her but she saw on his face that something was wrong.

"They... this is just an invitation... nonsense, since when am I afraid of a letter? Enough, don't worry, Shurka, it's not good for the baby."

Avraham had to report to the offices of the regional German headquarters. The doctor who checked him declared that he was fit and wrote it in a special book. But... fit for what?

"Don't ask," others hinted to him. "Here, every word is dangerous. Every question comes with punishment."

The answer was fit enough to do forced labor for the Third Reich. Along with other men—neighbors from near and far, Jews and Poles alike—Avraham was sent to work in a work camp near the city of Ostrow Lubelski.

He was stripped of his clothes and fur coat and dressed in rough gray cotton, with a cloth cap on his head. He had become a number on an infinite list. In one fell swoop Avraham, the respected merchant, had become a nameless man.

"Why do you worry, woman?" he placated Shurka when he

returned from the camp.

"You look thinner."

"I am lucky."

"You are a prisoner."

"Quiet, woman," he hushed, "it's just an open work camp, not a prison, I can leave and see you as much as I want."

But Shurka was not calm. She saw her husband growing thinner, his face graying, and understood that something bad was happening to him. He was losing hope. His spirit had fallen.

While Avraham was paving roads for the German army, lugging rocks and spreading wet sand, Shurka stayed behind, the burden of the house on her shoulders. She fed the chickens, stored the potatoes away in the cellar, pickled cucumbers, kneaded dough for noodles and prayed for her husband's safety.

"Mama," Irena would call to her at night, "I'm scared," and Shurka would wrap her daughter in a blanket and move her to the bed she had shared with Avraham.

"I want my father," whispered Irena.

"He will come soon."

"Papa..."

"Don't cry..." and Shurka would embrace her daughter. "Look how happy we are. We have the house, we have a yard, we have each other, and Papa will come as soon as he can. He was here just three days ago and told you a story."

"But Papa is far away."

"Far but close. The important thing is he is able to come to us."

"I want Papa."

"Did you see that?" Shurka tried to distract her. "Our storks have come back to their nest on the electric pole. Tomorrow put a bowl of water out for them so that they know that they are welcome here."

Irena finally fell asleep and Shurka stroked her cheek and said a silent prayer: *"Please, my lord, let there be peace and let our lives go back to being the way that they were so that we can go back to being the people we were."*

8.

One evening Shurka, who was sleeping in the double bed with little Irena, was startled awake by the whinnying of horses. She hurried over to the window and saw a cart harnessed to two horses that had stopped near their house. Her heart skipped a beat. Lord, what now?

She hung beside the window, afraid to move.

"My Shurka," she heard her husband's voice, but still she did not move. Did he, God forbid, come bearing bad news?

Avraham got down from the wagon, wrapped in a patched woolen blanket.

"Is everything alright?" She held him close in a powerful embrace. "Are my parents safe? Your parents? My sister?"

"They are ok, everyone is in good health."

"So, what...?"

"Everything is fine," he answered her in his way, but his face was clouded by worry.

"How is everything fine? You are here... the cart that you brought, and the two horses... Did something happen? Tell me quickly!"

"Enough questions, listen to me Sarah, we must hurry."

"Where?"

"I thought of everything, I don't want you staying here alone, I came to take you."

Shurka withdrew. She suddenly felt dizzy. "Why? What

happened?"

"There are rumors..."

"Rumors of what? What happened?"

"Don't ask too much. You can't stay here. You shouldn't be living alone in times like these. We must stay together."

"Leave everything? But this is our home!"

"It's only temporary," Avraham softened his voice. "Until we understand what's going on."

The sound of Irena crying reached their ears as she looked for her mother who had disappeared from the warm bed.

"But..."

"No 'buts', we will get you back to your village. It's all worked out, your parents are expecting you. Hurry, I have to be back at the camp before dawn."

He did not tell her what terrible fate awaited those who dared to leave the camp without permission. The Polish guard he had bribed said his shift was over at six in the morning. He would have to hurry.

"To leave..."

"I don't know for how long. Hurry, we must go!"

Shurka's face twisted in sorrow. She loved their home, the marigolds, the apple and chestnut trees, and the bubbling of the small stream that flowed by.

"To squeeze into my parents' little house with the girl and the baby that will soon be born? Are you sure it will be easier there?"

"Listen, my dear," Avraham leaned towards his wife, "there's no choice, there are rumors that they have started to shoot Jews in the street and..."

"And you always said that the Germans were a cultured people."

"And I was wrong, very wrong. Listen, I was told that not

far from Lublin, at a crossroads, they shot a Jewish family, just like that, without a trial, just because they identified them as Jews. This isn't just a matter of displacement anymore. I think this is the right thing to do, to be together. A family needs to be united at a time like this."

He spoke in a soft, quiet voice so that Irena would not hear.

"What will become of us," cried Shurka, and Irena woke up. "Is that Papa's voice?"

"Where's my girl?" Avraham hurried to her.

"Papa," she reached out her small hands to him, "I missed you! Where were you? Did you know that yesterday I fed the chickens and they pecked my finger? And I didn't even cry?"

"I am happy, that means you're a big girl," Avraham pulled her to him. "I was far, far away, beyond the mountains, but I thought of you the whole time."

"Me and Alinka want you to tell us a story"

"Not now, maybe tomorrow."

"Why are you sad, Papa?" And Avraham could hardly hold back his tears. He did not know how much longer he would be able to protect his beloved family.

"Sarah," he turned to his wife who was still hesitating, "We have to get moving."

"You mean that we will leave immediately? Tonight?"

"Yes." Avraham stroked her cheek. "It's not good for you to be here alone. I don't know where they will move our camp."

Shurka knew, in her heart, that he was right. She had seen the houses of the Jewish farmers in the surrounding area steadily emptying out. The women whose husbands had been sent to work camps worried about staying alone in their homes, left to their fate. They bundled up their belongings, and advanced towards the Russian border. Whole villages had been abandoned by their residents. Every so often a family of refugees came through, planning to cross the border. She heard the people talking about what was happening in Warsaw. The merchants who stopped in her village described the power of the German army, the huge tanks that flattened everything and the motor-cyclists who shot anyone who crossed their path like rats...

"Let's go, we have to hurry," Avraham urged his wife, "choose what to bring, but be careful - the cart won't be able to carry everything."

"How will I know?"

"Come on, take only what is necessary, the rest I will come back and sell when I can. Who knows what the day will bring."

"Just don't forget our photographs," said Shurka. "Memories are also precious."

They went to pack. They took winter coats out of the storage cupboard, boots and shoes, and a few tools and quilts. They rolled up the new carpet and took the candlesticks and silver-ware. They packed prayer books, the potatoes, cabbage and the carrots that had been stored in the basement, the photo album, papers and documents. When they finished, Avraham told Shurka he had to settle a few more things. She waited for him in the little kitchen. Through the window she saw him digging in the yard as he unearthed a heavy chest containing the trea-sure intended for times like these.

At the last minute, Shurka removed the sign that Avraham had made in the early days with their names, "Sarah Avraham and Irena" written on it. The sign was big, with space enough for the many children they had hoped to raise here.

"Mama, we have to take my toys, too." Irena stood in the entrance to the kitchen, dragging a big box of toys behind her. Shurka turned away from the window and shook her head sadly.

"I'm sorry, princess, there isn't space. We will go and later Papa will bring them."

"Can I bring just my Alinka doll? She is afraid to stay alone."

Shurka hugged Irena. She knew that the salty taste in her mouth was from the tears flowing down her cheeks, wetting her neck and her hair.

"Why are you crying?"

"Because I am sad to leave the house."

"Mama is crying," said Irena, "look, Alinka doll isn't crying."

"Alinka doll is right," said Shurka, "we must smile, keep our heads up and smile. We must be happy with what we have."

She felt a wound open up in her heart but she smiled. She knew that she would never see her beloved house again. She stroked the walls that she had painted with her own hands, the bookshelf that remained standing, filled with books, the bedroom door that had seen those days of love.

She felt as though she had grown up all at once, that she was not afraid.

From that day on she found that she could not cry. Tears made her weak. Gave her away. She had to stay strong, and steady as a rock for her family and for the wellbeing of her children.

When they finished and everything appeared ready, Avraham signaled to Shurka to come out after him. She bundled up little Irena, who had fallen asleep on the rug, and gave one last glance around the house that had known only happiness. At the last moment she stuffed the big silver cup for Elijah the prophet into her pocket and picked up her sleeping child. Irena opened her eyes. She did not ask why or where, and she no longer cried or complained about the hard road or the cold. Tight in her mother's arms, she fell back asleep.

"Look at our daughter," Shurka whispered to Avraham, "it's as though she grew up all at once."

"All of us have, Sarah, but, remember, it's all temporary. We will add a second floor to the house for our many children yet."

Shurka sat beside Avraham, facing back toward her village as the cart moved ahead. She looked at the house for as long as she could, preserving its memory. Slowly it was swallowed up into the darkness. She could no longer see the white fence, and into that darkness the windows, the roof, the chimney, and the whole house disappeared from their sight. Forever.

She did not know that it, along with other houses from the village, would soon be turned into a mound of ashes, that looters would rip the lace off the curtains she had lovingly embroidered, tear down the cloth lamp that Avraham had hung, take Irena's box of blocks, and burn the family photographs that they had left behind in haste. Nothing would remain of their home but its memory.

9.

"Thank God you're here, we were already worried," Taiba greeted them as the cart stopped by the dark house.

"Give me little Irena," said Yaakov Mendel.

Shurka got down from the cart and handed over her sleeping daughter. Both Yaakov Mendel joined Avraham, and wordlessly helped him unload the wagon.

They had to hurry - Avraham could not be late to return to the camp and he still had to bury his chest somewhere hidden so it would not, God forbid, fall into the hands of greedy neighbors. The Jews knew that as soon as they left, the Poles would loot their homes, and try to find where the Jews had buried their gold rings.

They brought the chest down to the basement, put a sack of potatoes on top of it and surrounded it with old clothes and shoes that smelled of sweat. When they had finished, everyone gathered in the little kitchen. Taiba prepared an aromatic tea and served cookies. Nobody spoke.

The girl's cries suddenly pierced the night.

"Alinka doll! Where are you Alinka? I want my doll!" Shurka heard Irena crying.

Shurka hurried to the crying child.

"What happened, sweetheart?" She found Irena sitting at the edge of the bed, her hands outstretched.

"Mama, my doll, I want my doll. Where is she?"

Grandpa Yaakov Mendel hurried to the wagon, searching and searching, Avraham took a lantern and checked the yard, the path, the entrance to the house, but Alinka doll was nowhere to be found.

"Maybe she fell along the way," said Shurka.

"We will look for it tomorrow," said Yaakov Mendel.

"No, please don't leave her alone, she's scared," cried Irena.

"Don't cry," Aunt Alinka comforted her. "Tomorrow we will make a new doll together. I have lots of silk and velvet and we can dress her like a queen."

"I don't want a new doll, I want my Alinka," Irena sobbed.

Shurka tried to calm her, but little Irena wailed.

"I think that Alinka doll was homesick and decided to go back to our house," Avraham tried to calm his daughter. "Don't worry, I promise you I will go back there and look for her."

"Yes, she will wait for you there," said Shurka and held her daughter close in a warm embrace.

"You will see, soon, God willing, when we get home, she will be there. You will find her sitting next to the window waiting for you."

"I want to go home, I want my Alinka, please take me home Mama," Irena cried. Shurka stroked her hair and sang her a song about forget-me-not flowers that grow in the snowy mountains of Poland, and about a child that lost his way in the forest until a kindly bear took pity on him, gave him milk, and showed him the way home. Taiba watched the two of them and tried to hide her tears. After Irena finally fell back asleep, Shurka went to the window, that same window with the double-paned glass where she used to sit and watch the trees and the forests and get to know the world.

Outside, silence prevailed. A light wind blew through the

treetops. In the complete darkness she could not see the lights of the village where her house was.

"Who knows," she whispered, possibly to herself, "if we will ever return to how things were..."

"Times are tough," said Aunt Alinka. "We must prepare for the worst."

"Enough with this talk," Taiba hugged her. "In times like these, we must remain hopeful. Enough crying. We are alive, and that's a lot."

Avraham parted, kissing his wife again and again and promising to visit the moment he was able.

"Look after the treasure that is here, in your belly, my darling," he said, and hurried to the wagon. She heard the wheels turning on the path and the neighing of the horses. Avraham disappeared.

Now Yaakov Mendel and Taiba's home, which stood at the crossroads at the edge of the village of Nowa Jedlanka, housed Shurka and Irena, Shurka's parents, her three siblings, Aunt Alinka and Uncle Yaakov Mendel and other relatives who had left their villages near Warsaw and found refuge at the home of their family.

The men tried to extract some yield from the stubborn earth in order to feed everyone, and the women did the cooking. They learned to prepare a lot from the little they had. They were required to bring what they produced to Lucian the drunk, the mayor of the village on behalf of the Germans, who passed the supplies on to the Germans, and left himself a little of everything to sell at exorbitant prices.

"Wonderful soup."

"Really?" laughed Shurka. "Just so you know, I made this wonderful soup from one potato and two carrots."

"And I learned how to make a fancy dessert from berries that I found not far from the house," boasted Aunt Alinka.

For little Irena, these days felt festive.

Grandma Taiba found Shurka's old doll in the basement, and Shurka sewed a blue silk dress for her and placed her in Irena's hands.

"This isn't my Alinka," Irena protested.

"It's Alinka," said Shurka. "When we get back to our house, Alinka and Alinka can be best friends."

Irena was surrounded by family. Saba Yaakov Mendel made her a flute from birch wood, Aunt Alinka knit her an orange hat and gloves, and her visiting cousins would take her to run around the field across from the house. At night, Grandma Taiba would tell her favorite stories.

One morning, the son of their neighbors, Shimon, who had been in love with Shurka when they were children and played together in the field, came to the house. He stood in the doorway, embarrassed, holding a birch-wood bed he had made for Alinka.

"Thank you, Shim'leh," said Shurka and Shimon blushed. He still remembered being rejected by Shurka. He would not try again, as she was a married woman.

"I saw your little Irena... she looks like you."

"You think so? People say she looks like Avraham, my husband."

"She looks like you. Sweet, as I remember you. I see that you are expecting..." Shimon blushed.

"Yes," said Shurka, "Soon... soon I will have two children." She added, quietly, "Times are tough. I am bringing this baby into a terrible world."

"Don't speak like that," said Yaakov Mendel who was teaching Irena to write.

"He's right, you will see that, God willing, everything will work out," said Shimon. "Soon your husband will return, all the men will return and the skies over Poland will clear up."

"Amen to that, one hundred times Amen."

"And I... I thought that maybe," Shimon's face reddened, "if you want, I can make a cradle for the baby that will soon be born."

"A cradle? My God, I had completely forgotten! You see what is happening to us? Everything was taken from us. They stole the cow, the crops, and the chickens are so frightened they hardly lay..."

"If you need anything..."

"Thank you, you really are a good neighbor. The baby will come soon and then we'll see."

She stroked her belly and thought, maybe when he comes into the world, all this evil will be behind them. "Are you afraid like me?" she asked the little one. "Do you also have trouble sleeping at night?"

Shurka missed Avraham. She missed their evening walks in the village, Friday nights when he would sing Sabbath songs in his deep voice, the warm hands that held her so lovingly, the whinnying of the horses that signaled his return home.

She knew that she had to stay strong. After all, they were lucky - she could not complain. The family had stayed together, crowded, but together. Healthy.

"You see how we're getting by," said Taiba after Shurka's first month staying in her parents' home. "It will be alright, believe me that everything will be fine, we just must be patient."

Shurka no longer knew whether to heed her parents' comforting words or Paritz Luboskowitz's warnings, or her sense that it was not good to sit idly by. She also knew that she could not do much in her current state, with the baby in her womb already hinting at his intentions to come out.

One night, Shurka woke up in alarm. There were cries coming from the room next to theirs. She hurried to the room and found her mother lying on her bed, her face buried in her pillow as she wept. Beside her stood her sister, Zipa.

"What happened to Mama?" Shurka asked and Yaakov Mendel hurried to get her out of the room and told her that bitter news had arrived in the night. Uncle Yitzhak, Aunt Fruma's husband, had been killed.

"Uncle Yitzhak? Why? What happened to him? Why is Mama shouting?"

Yitzhak was one of Taiba's brothers and Shurka's favorite uncle. When he would came to visit, he would teach her the names of trees, make her spinning tops and teach her to play the comb...

"He was on his way from Ostrow Lubelski to the nearby village, and on the way they arrested him and..."

"What happened to him?"

"They... animals... they just shot him... like a dog. Didn't ask, didn't say a word, and boom, animals!" Papa hissed through his clenched teeth.

"But why?"

"The Germans, they don't need a reason to shoot a Jew. They left his body lying there on the ground, took the horse and cart and disappeared," said Yaakov Mendel. "Now go back to sleep, we must be strong for Mama."

Shurka ran her hand across her round belly and in that moment came to a decision. She would name her son after her beloved Uncle Yitzhak. Yitzhak, she mumbled the name and stroked her belly where the baby was wiggling. Yitzhak, the beloved son of our foremother Sarah and our forefather Abraham.

Only as the dawn broke did she manage to fall asleep.

Winter 1941.

Irena was three years old. She would sit by the window and much like her mother Shurka before her, would look out at the world. Sometimes she would help knead the dough.

The sky was dark with heavy clouds. Although the winter was harsh, it was warm in the little home of the Shidlovsky family. It smelled of baked bread and fried onions. Shurka felt the baby moving inside her, hinting that it would soon arrive.

The German army began to appear in the villages. They did not enter but simply passed through, heading east. The German soldiers, tanks and cannons moving toward the Russian border became a common sight in the villages. Gestapo soldiers in black uniforms also came through in need of supplies. They eyed the peasants' property and took cows and horses from the fields toward "the war effort."

Every now and then a soldier in black uniform would come through the village, with shiny boots and an expressionless face. He would interrogate villagers and make lists of who among the farmers believed in Jesus and who did not pray to him. Then he would sit with Lucian the drunk and together they would go over the lists. These were Gestapo soldiers making lists regarding the Jewish population.

In the house of Yaakov Mendel and Taiba, nobody spoke aloud about what was to come. They had to remain optimistic and believe that it was all just passing clouds. Soon a new person would be joining their happy family. It was not a time to worry.

Yitzhak was born on a cold night, with snow piled high on the paths outside and covering the windows.

When the contractions began, Yaakov Mendel hurried to harness the wagon to the one horse that remained and galloped to the work camp to summon Avraham.

"Impossible," said the Pole, but Yaakov Mendel saw that his eyes sparkled and he bribed the Polish guard to allow Avraham to leave for a few hours.

For fear of the Germans, they did not call the midwife and Taiba promised that she knew exactly what needed to be done. After all, she had helped cousins and friends deliver their babies on multiple occasions. Taiba and Aunt Alinka helped Shurka deliver her baby. They knew exactly what to do and quietly gave Shurka instructions and encouragement. Before Avraham could get there, Yitzhak had arrived.

"Congratulations," they told her and laid the baby on her belly. She smiled at the baby who had joined the family and called Irena to come meet her baby brother. Irena held his tiny hand and kissed his fingers.

"He's cute!"

"Like you," laughed Shurka.

"The most important thing is that he will have good luck," said Taiba and hurried to the other room to wipe her tears. Taiba stroked Yitzhak's cheek. Who knew what would be the fate of this tiny baby.

For a time, joy returned to their home. It was as though the birth of Yitzhak had brought with it a sliver of hope.

Yitzhak was a delightful, beautiful baby. His face was smooth and clear. His dark eyes and freshness made the whole family melt. But he was also delicate and frail. He was smaller than other babies his age. He cried a great deal and did not nurse enough.

"Maybe because he can feel that I'm worried."

"Don't feel guilty," Taiba told her daughter.

"Of course, the months of this pregnancy were not easy like the first," said Avraham as he soothed his baby during the few precious hours that he was able to come.

"I am worried I don't have enough milk."

"Enough with the worries," Taiba said curtly. "You must rest more, laugh more and stop thinking bad thoughts. It is important for the baby."

"I am trying, but it's not bad thoughts that interfere with Yitzhak's feeding. Something is bothering him - he cries too much."

"Maybe you didn't eat properly. Tomorrow I will go to the market and trade the white lace table cloth for some fresh vegetables."

Shurka bounced the crying child and prayed for his well-being. Taiba made miracles in the kitchen and from the half chicken she managed to acquire she made a hearty stew that would last for several days. There was no milk to be had. The Germans had taken most of the cows. Only Avraham, who managed to get to the house in the middle of the night every so often to keep up his family's morale, was somehow able to bring some fresh milk for the baby, sometimes some carrots, half a cabbage, or even a tiny piece of meat.

"Where is it from?" Shurka asked her husband when he produced a bottle of milk from his pocket.

"Better you don't ask," Avraham smiled at her. So she did not ask. These days everything she had been taught seemed to be worthless. She should be content just to get what she needed and not ask too many questions. Everything they did was in order to survive. They could only hope that it was just a matter of time.

Avraham really was a magician. He managed to acquire what nobody else knew was possible; sometimes he would even bring cream or fresh eggs. They did not know that there would be many days in which Avraham would supply the food to his family and others in a way that only he knew. And the questions of how and from whom would not be asked.

Saba Yaakov Mendel would sneak an extra potato onto Shurka's plate.

"Eat, eat," he urged her, "you need your strength. We will manage." And Taiba knocked on the doors of their Polish neighbors, asking, begging, to try to bring fresh fruits and vegetables to the children.

10.

Avraham continued to go and visit his family, sometimes once a week, and sometimes only once a month. Every time he came, Shurka would look at him with concern. Each time he was paler and his eyes were dimmer. He always had a surprise in his pocket: two eggs, a red apple, a head of cabbage - and nobody asked any questions. "Mister Plenty," they joked, a nickname that would stick to him in the coming years. Little Irena, for whom he would sometimes even have a candy, called him "Papa Surprise."

And the rumors continued to pour in, worsening from one day to the next.

"Come with us, don't stay here," pleaded the refugees who passed not far from their house.

"You must get out! What will you do when they get here?" their neighbors warned, as they too began to flee.

But Shurka looked at her little Yitzhak and knew that he would not survive the journey. Maybe next year, she reasoned to herself, he will be stronger and we too can go to the eastern border.

"What are they trying to do?" Shurka asked the Paritz, who had come to visit her and bring her cream and cheese for the children.

"This is the scheme of that madman, Hitler," he explained to the family members who gathered to listen to what he had to say. "The Einsatzgruppen have joined forces with the German army - to clean Eastern Poland to make space for the people expelled from the west. The so-called 'relocate the population' operation."

"Which is to say he wants to clear all of us out of here?"

The Paritz nodded his head. "He wants to clear the area, to evict all the Jews and to settle others in your homes - it is the crazy plan of a madman. What do you intend to do?"

"To get out of here as soon as possible, after the winter," said Yaakov Mendel. "The baby is not yet strong enough."

They did not know that the discovery of Zyklon B would change everything, that the Germans had found a more efficient way to get rid of the Jews, and that they had begun to systematically wipe out the Jewish centers and ghettos.

When Yitzhak was three months old, family members from one of the nearby villages turned up at the house bringing bitter news.

"They are already shooting Jews in the streets," they reported. "They're calling it 'free rein.' Do you understand what that means?"

"You are exaggerating."

"Yesterday they shot my neighbor," said Shmuel Perlmutter, "this volcano is about to explode."

"How? Is there no law? No police?"

"They are the law, they are the police. And they have placed us outside the law. We heard that twenty people, all from one family, were shot in the street and the killers just kept on walking and laughing. They are saying it is just the beginning, that they have bigger plans. My dear people, save yourselves."

"But we have friends here..."

"Nobody is a friend. The Germans bought the Poles, and they will sell a Jew for a bottle of vodka. You cannot trust anybody."

Taiba looked at Shurka. "He's right. Lucian gave them organized lists of the Jews in the area. What will we do against the German army?"

"Leave. Many Jews have escaped to the Russian side," said Shmuel Perlmutter.

"But who says that there it will be any better?" asked Uncle Yaakov Mendel.

"Here it is the worst."

"We have to act immediately... afterwards who knows. We are leaving, we came to suggest that you come with us. To do nothing is not an option."

Shurka took Irena and went out to the yard. She did not want her daughter to hear the frightening things being said inside.

Devorah, Irena's younger sister, joined them. Her pretty face bore a look of great sadness. She had recently married the man she loved, Shamai Fishel, and together they dreamed of setting up a home and a family. But that dream appeared to be retreating further and further away.

In the evening, after the two children had gone to sleep, the family discussed their options: To wait. To leave after the winter. To stay. To trust in God?

The arguments went on for days.

Each possibility could have dire consequences.

"We should wait," said Yaakov Mendel. "Meanwhile the Germans haven't touched anybody in our area. They took what they needed. Anyways, in the village we are all equal - who can tell the difference between a Polish peasant and a Jewish peasant?"

"To wait for them to slaughter us, is that what you're suggesting?"

"Do you believe the stories? People are exaggerating."

"I don't trust anybody," said Taiba. "Life here has become hard. It breaks my heart to say it but I think we have to leave... and the sooner the better. They say that in Ostrow, Jews from all over are grouping together. Maybe there, together, we will be safe."

"Mama," interrupted Shurka, "in Ostrow Lubelski before the war there were only 1500 Jews, a third of the population. Now there are 3000, double. Do you understand what that means?"

"It means that the Germans are gathering the Jews together. What is the goal?"

"To take our chances and stay here?"

"To voluntarily move into a ghetto?"

"What's the matter? Ostrow isn't Warsaw, and it is an open ghetto."

"For now... but later, who knows?"

Devorah held her new husband's hand and tears streamed down her cheeks. Would they have to spend their honeymoon in a ghetto?

"I do not intend to move there," he whispered to her.

"So what will you do?"

"Join Yehiel Greenspan."

"Who?"

"Yehiel Greenspan, from the Greenspan family, the horse merchants?" asked Uncle Yaakov Mendel. "I know him, an excellent young man."

"He and others like him escaped from their work camp and settled in the Parczew Forest."

Shurka grew anxious. To move to the forest and the marshes with two small children?

"There? To the forest? You mean... that we would go live there?"

"Yes, I heard about Jews who ran away to the forests and joined up with Yehiel. That's where we will go, and that's where we will celebrate our honeymoon."

"Shhh," Devorah quieted him and pointed to Shurka.

"No," said Yaakov Mendel decisively. "We are one family. Whatever we decide, we will decide together. All of us, together."

"I am in favor of going east. Talk to your mother - she is a logical woman."

"Do what is right for you," whispered Shurka to Devorah when she understood her brother-in-law's plan. "Yitzhak is not strong enough. He won't survive the difficult journey." Yaakov Mendel looked at his daughter and shook his head.

"We must wait. Maybe we should consult with Avraham. He will know what to do."

Devorah looked at Shurka, quietly cradling little Yitzhak.

"As soon as our little Yitzhak becomes stronger, we will go," said Taiba. "We should start preparing ourselves."

"How?" cried Aunt Alinka in despair. "They even took our horses!"

"Don't worry, I will be the horse," her husband tried to make her laugh and began running about the room whinnying, and everyone burst out laughing.

"As long as we can still laugh, it will be alright," Yaakov Mendel joined in the general merriment. "We will manage. Your friend Paritz Luboskowitz promised to help us. When your Avraham comes for a visit we will plan our next steps."

Reaching a collective decision infused them with a new optimism that they desperately needed. They would wait for the winter to pass and set off.

The next Sabbath, the day of rest, their plans changed abruptly.

That morning the skies were blue and bright, white butterflies fluttered around the flowers, Saba Yaakov Mendel told little Irena a story and Shurka fed little Yitzhak in her lap. He learned to suck the finger she would dip in the little bit of milk that their friend the Paritz had brought them.

The tranquility of a holy day.

Tranquility that was suddenly disrupted.

The sounds of soldiers approaching, the echo of their steps on the paving stones made the family's blood run cold. Someone somewhere shouted and someone else replied. Their cries were unmistakable.

"Jews!" The soldiers shouted. "There are Jews there." And the steps got nearer.

They just looked at one another in stunned silence, not daring to ask or say a thing that might betray their fear. Crammed together as a single unit, they prayed in their hearts to someone who might save them, who would rescue them from what might happen. Then, all at once, the tranquility of the holy day was ruined.

They heard it - there was a burst of gunfire and then silence, as though the world had frozen. A split second passed before they heard the shouts that followed. Still frozen where they were, they listened. Afterwards they heard the voices of soldiers calling to one another, celebrating some despicable victory, and then getting farther away. One of them sang a cheerful song and his friends joined in.

Several more minutes passed before Saba Yaakov Mendel dared to look out the window. He motioned to Uncle Yaakov

Mendel to come and he pressed his face to the glass, held his head with two hands and tears streamed down his face.

"What happened?" Taiba asked her husband.

"Who was shot? What happened?" added Aunt Alinka.

"Not now," said Yaakov Mendel and moved the women away from the window.

"What happened Yaakov Mendel? Tell me!"

"There is no time for talk. Take Ruska and Shlomo and Shurka and the babies and all of you go down to the basement."

"But what's going on..."

"Immediately!" He raised his voice. "Stay there until I tell you to come out."

"And what about you Papa?" asked Shurka.

"Stay completely quiet. Do as I say, and quickly!"

"Yaakov Mendel..." Taiba tried to get close to the window but he stopped her. All she managed to see was a *tallit,* or prayer shawl, stained with blood.

"Who... God, Yaakov Mendel, who did they shoot?"

"Don't ask questions, there isn't time. Hurry, woman." Taiba knew by the color of his face and the furious tone of his voice that something terrible had happened and that it was better not to ask.

She hurried over to Shurka and snatched little Yitzhak from her hands. He immediately began to cry, searching for the drop of milk that had been taken from him. For a moment Shurka tried to protest, to take the baby back but Taiba instructed her to hurry after her.

The whole family crowded together in the basement as Yaakov Mendel had ordered. They were clutching each other and weeping.

Yitzhak, as though understanding, did not cry and little Irena stayed glued to her mother. She knew, without their having to explain, that she must stay quiet, not ask questions or get in the way. Children understand. They know how to grow up quickly.

An hour later both Yaakov Mendels returned to the house. Shurka would always remember the sound of their steps. Heavy. Slow. A bad sign. They went down to the basement and sat down heavily. Their hands were covered in mud and their faces bore great sadness. Silence prevailed in the basement and nobody dared to ask what they had seen.

"It's Leibka..." whispered Yaakov Mendel at last. Nobody dared speak. They listened.

"They broke in and started shooting, as though these people were sick dogs, in the middle of prayers."

"Where was this God that they were praying to?" Taiba clutched her face in her hands, only her sobs breaking the silence. "That's what I want to know - God, who is in the sky has abandoned us..."

"And the children?" Shurka shuddered. "What about children?"

Yaakov Mendel covered his face with his hands.

"Speak."

"Everyone who was there... the three children, Shulik, Yosef and Mordecai. They shot them all. They didn't take pity on the little ones."

"And Miriam and Shimon? What about them?"

"At least they survived. They were lucky they weren't home just then. They had gone out to look for food... it was terrible. They looted the house and when they finished they destroyed everything..." His voice faltered.

Nobody knew what would happen next. So they waited in the basement for several hours, crammed in next to one another, until the evening. Both Yaakov Mendels went back up and checked the surroundings.

"It's alright, you can come up," said Yaakov Mendel. "It looks like they won't be back today. But tomorrow... who knows...? They say that one of the Poles pointed out their house."

"It's Lucian, he's been handing over Jews from the area for a while now. He has his eye on us, that drunken good-for-nothing."

"That's what I said," exclaimed Taiba. "We can't trust anybody, only ourselves! The number of collaborators is growing. It is a miracle that we were saved."

The four who had been murdered were brought to be buried in the field beside their house. Beside the big pit, Shimon said the Kaddish and Miriam read the poems of the Jewish poet Julian Tuwim.

What is homeland?
"I believe that homeland is - the world!
But I was badly cheated -
This homeland is the sad yard
That I have not visited since long ago!"

And every word that was said was an arrow in each of their hearts.

11.

In the month of January 1942, one week after the pogrom against their neighbors, the Shidlovsky family abandoned the house and the village where they had been born and raised. They finally understood.

The arguments ceased; the Germans had made it apparent that there was no way out. They had to take action rather than wait around for the next attack.

It was clear to them that the shocking murder that had taken place in front of their house, in broad daylight, without anyone's lifting a finger was a turning point. The writing on the wall indicated that people could not hide their heads in the sand. There was no doubt that to stay in the village in their comfortable home was to put themselves in great danger and hand themselves to the murderers.

They knew that some of the families who had been living in nearby villages had fled to the Parczew Forest and were hiding there. Their plan, however, was to move to the ghetto that had been established in Ostrow Lubelski, to reunite with their relatives and to connect up with the large Jewish community that they knew well. There, they believed, they would feel secure. There was safety in numbers.

They did not say a word about their plans to their Polish friends. From the moment when they finally understood that they were allowed be killed, and the Germans were handsomely paying those who informed, they realized that any friend could be an enemy. Sometimes they would see Lucian peering at them, and they knew that the sooner they could leave the better. The world of 1942 was not a safe place for them.

There were many relatives living in Ostrow Lubelski who had agreed to host them and to help them get organized and find an apartment. But the weather was harsh. Snowstorms raged outside and the temperature dropped to below zero.

It was agreed that Taiba and Yaakov Mendel would move first, see what the situation was like... if they could find a suitable apartment, Aunt Alinka and Uncle Yaakov Mendel and the two children, Shlomo and Ruska, would join them.

Shurka and the two small children would go to live on the estate of their friend Paritz Luboskowitz, who was willing to host them in one of the abandoned pavilions on his large property. They were worried that, God forbid, little Yitzhak might not survive the winter.

The large house of the Paritz was some distance from the village. They would be able to hide there from the eyes of the Germans or the Poles, at least until they could find themselves a safe place to live in Ostrow Lubelski.

A week later Taiba and Yaakov Mendel returned with everything worked out.

"There is an apartment. Nothing fancy, a little cramped," said Taiba. "But it is a decent place, and in these hard times, it may as well be a palace."

How do you abandon a home? How do you leave the warm nest in which the love of Taiba and Yaakov Mendel had grown - the house where their children had been born and raised, where they had married and given their parents grandchildren - the house which contained all of their happy and sad memories?

Years later, Shurka would report: "After it was decided that there was no other choice but to leave the house, my mama became efficient and practical. She encouraged all of us. She said, 'Don't sigh, and stop with your laments. A house is just a few walls and a floor. Family is what's important. We love one another and as long as we stay together nothing bad will happen.' And we all clung to her optimism."

The family started to quietly prepare, without attracting any attention. Each of them packed his own most precious belongings into a suitcase. Photographs were bundled together with blankets, winter coats, wool hats, scarves and shoes. Yaakov Mendel said that they needed to be equipped for the cold winter which might be their biggest threat.

Documents and deeds of ownership of the house and the land were packed into big glass jars and buried away in the cellar. Under the duress of the present circumstances, it was decided not to take the Torah books with them but to bury them too in the cellar. They packed the books with great care, wrapping them in oilcloth then in waterproof sheets. Then they dug a large pit. Yaakov Mendel indicated the best spot to put them so they would not, God forbid, get wet.

They lowered them into the pit in the dark of night and were careful not to damage them, God forbid. As gently as if they were babies, they covered the pit with wooden boards and placed a large barrel on top so that when the time came they could rescue and restore them.

"God, if you are there, keep our books safe," whispered Shurka, "just like you looked after little Moses in his basket."

A few hours later the house was empty of its inhabitants. Only the big pear tree remained standing, as if shielding the house with its large branches. And above it was the empty storks' nest.

While Taiba, Yaakov Mendel, Devorah, Shlomo and Ruska were heading east towards Ostrow, Avraham took care to safely deliver his family to the large estate of the Paritz.

"Are you sure?" Avraham asked when he suggested that Shurka and the little ones hide at his place. The Paritz answered that on his estate, Shurka would be safe.

"But I am also thinking of you - what if they find out?"

"Why should they find out?"

"They are looking for Jews."

"I'm not frightened. They respect me. After all, they see me as a nobleman of the chosen race."

They left early in the morning, even before the farmers had woken up to do the morning milking. A few days earlier, he had transferred some blankets, warm clothes and a little food to a hiding place.

"So that you will have enough for a few days," he explained. "I hope that very soon the spring will come and we can reunite with the family."

They stealthily made their way without saying a word, the children clutched tightly in their arms, trying not to make a sound or wake any of the members of Paritz Luboskowitz' family who were not privy to the secret.

This time Shurka did not look back. She knew that her childhood home could not protect them any longer.

"We forgot Elijah's cup! How will we celebrate the Passover holiday without it?" Shurka panicked when they were already on their way. Avraham promised that he would return as soon as possible to her parents' house and take the decorated silver cup - before the neighbors raided their belongings that had been left behind.

"No," she said. "I don't want you to take any chances. Your life is more precious than a cup."

When the village was already behind them, Avraham and Sarah stood and looked.

"Go forth..." whispered Avraham.

"To a land that I will show you," Shurka completed the sentence.

"Where do you want us to go?" Avraham shouted at the sky.

"Why is Papa shouting?" asked little Irena, and Avraham lifted up his daughter and gave her a kiss.

At that moment, during the winter of 1942, while all of Poland was covered by a blanket of snow, Shurka, Avraham and their children became refugees, without a home. From that moment on they would not find respite, a secure place free from worry.

They would be moving between one hidden place to another in order to survive.

12.

When they entered the little wooden hut on Paritz Luboskowitz' estate and Avraham lit the lantern to show them the hiding spot, Shurka had to restrain herself from bursting into tears. She knew that this place, though crowded, dark and damp, was preferable to the house they had left behind where they had been in real danger.

Baby Yitzhak snuggled in close to her, trying to nurse, and began to cry.

"What can I do, my baby? I have no milk," she sighed. "My poor child, what will become of you?"

Outside a snowstorm raged. Only a little light made its way into their crowded hut and the wind threatened to blow the roof off from over their heads. In the absence of beds, they spread out the sheets that they had brought with them on the moldy, straw-covered floor, covered themselves with their wool blankets and fell asleep in an embrace.

Little Yitzhak was quiet, as though he understood that he had to make do with a light meal.

Shurka woke up very early to say goodbye to Avraham, who had to return to the work camp before daybreak. Little Irena also woke up. She looked at the crumbling wooden walls, heard the whistle of the wind that shook the little wooden house and snuggled in closer to her mother. Shurka lit the lantern that the Paritz had left them and brought her a cup of hot tea and a slice of rye bread.

"You understand, Alinka," Shurka heard Irena talking to her doll. "You have to be a good girl and be grateful for what we have because others don't even have this."

"That's how I was," Irena would remember many years later. "I was an attentive child. I didn't ask, didn't demand, didn't get in the way. Everything they gave me was good. Children pick up on situations quickly and they adapt. The truth was that I didn't understand what was happening. I didn't ask and they didn't tell me, but I knew that from then on, this was my role, to be helpful by being quiet."

Little Irena already knew so much about life and the world, and she was only a young girl. A little girl whose rights were being taken away from her and who was forced to adapt, to be satisfied with what there was, if there was anything at all.

They stayed at the estate for just a few weeks until the snow melted and it became a little warmer outside.

Shurka counted the days until they could reunite with her family. There was always the concern that someone from the estate would sniff around and discover that Jews were hiding there. The Poles were already searching for Jews to hand them over to the Gestapo. They had to remain in the little wooden hut at all hours of the day. Only when darkness fell could they go out a little.

What do you do in a hiding place for so many hours, and how do you stay quiet?

Stories, Shurka and Irena learned, in the days when they were hidden away in the hut, became important companions in times like these. Mama told story after story. About princesses and evil witches, of a boy made of wood named Pinocchio and about Little Red Riding Hood. The story that Irena loved most was about a pine tree that was unhappy with its spiky needles. Asking to replace them, the tree was given glass leaves, but these broke; later he received golden leaves that were stolen by robbers until the pine begged for his original needles back.

Irena listened and asked Shurka to tell the story over and over. And there were others... about the kid goat, the ravens, the oaks. Irena listened and listened and always wanted more. In this way the hours passed until evening when they would wrap up little Yitzhak and go out to the yard to take in some fresh air.

They would walk around a little, pluck fresh leaves, breathe in the sweet air, and return to their hiding place. Sometimes they would find a jar of jam or a loaf of bread beside the door to the hut, and sometimes a jug of milk that Shurka would heat and give to Yitzhak who had begun to smile.

"Until when, Avraham?" Shurka asked her husband when he came once in a while for a rushed nighttime visit.

"A few more days. Patience, meanwhile you are in a safe place."

"A safe place? But it is forbidden to hide Jews, even Lyudmila, the Paritz's wife doesn't know we're here. He is a good man and he is doing a lot for us. But what will happen if it is found out that he is giving Jews refuge in his home?"

"He knows what he's doing. He has important connections, and nobody will touch him. You must wait. A few more weeks and the weather will get a bit better and we can move on."

One day Shurka looked at Yitzhak. He was weak and barely cried. His eyes were sad. He was a child who had learned that the world was not a safe place in which to grow up.

"Lay down, my little one, lay down and rest," Shurka sang to him quietly, "*Do not cry bitterly / your mother sits by your* side / protecting you from evil / The jackal wails outside, the wind blows... Lay down, my little one..." She rocked the child, her warm tears wetting her face, and she thought that maybe she had run out of strength. Maybe she would not be able to protect her baby from the evil in the world. Maybe all of these words were just lies that were meant to obscure the truth.

But she went on. To tell stories. To sing to her children, and soothe them with her pleasant voice. She sang to them about cyclamens blooming and storks returning in the spring. Yitzhak fell asleep in her lap. He, like his sister, had already learned to be satisfied with meager portions of food.

Shurka also invented games to pass the time. They counted the stalks of straw that they found in the corners of the hut and arranged them in packages and she taught Irena some addition and subtraction. They would sell one another stones that they found in the yard and practice sums. Irena already knew how to count to one thousand. Sometimes, Shurka would teach her daughter about the biblical Avraham and Sarah and tell her stories from the book of Genesis.

The time passed slowly - too slowly. In her heart she was worried. The cold penetrated their bones and they waited. Why? Any day someone could break in and shoot them.

"We have to move," Shurka told her husband again. "Look at our little Yitzhak. He is so weak and small. We have to see a doctor. I am worried that he's not well."

Avraham had not told his wife that the situation in the ghetto had gotten worse. It was still open, but thousands of Jews were crowding there, living in harsh conditions and the doctors were helpless. Diseases broke out throughout the city and there was no medicine to be had.

"Until when? We need to see a doctor."

"I want to be with my parents and my siblings, it's hard here." And Avraham promised her that soon, just another week, two weeks at the latest, the situation would improve. The spring would come and she could reunite with her family. It was impossible to go anywhere with a baby in this weather; the snow was still falling, and there were no horses or wagons to use. The Germans had taken everything.

"It's hard for me here alone," whispered Shurka, wiping away a tear and releasing a long sigh. Avraham understood. But he felt the time was not yet right.

"Everyone misses you," he hugged his little family. "Soon we will all be together."

When the month of April came and the sun peeked out from time to time and the skies cleared up, Avraham brought his wife and two children towards Ostrow Lubelski. They walked all night and arrived in the early hours of the morning.

Shurka recalled the city well from the days when she had studied sewing there and lived at the home of her aunt and uncle. She remembered the pretty commercial street, the boulevard full of trees, and the big synagogue with its menorah. But this was not the pretty place of years past; Ostrow looked like a city whose beauty had faded and grown old too soon.

13.

Jews settled in the town of Ostrow Lubelski starting in the second half of the 18th century. By the end of that century, the town already had an independent Jewish community and some of the first known rabbis from there include Rabbi Shimshon Zelig Bar Yosef, author of *"Tzeutot Chen"*, as well as Rabbi Elyakum Getz. In the mid-20th century, a stone synagogue was built in the town.

In the period between the two world wars, most of the Jews retained their traditional occupations, and made a living primarily from trade and the local garment and baking industries. They lived well and had good relations with their Christian neighbors.

In the 1920s, local branches of Zionist movements were established in the town, including *Hahalutz*, *Hashomer Hatzair*, and *Beitar*. *Agudat Israel* and The Bund also had local offices, and there were a number of active Hebrew libraries.

Before World War II broke out, there were about 1500 Jews living in the town, about a third of its population.

The town was occupied by the Germans during the first week of the war. On the 17th of September 1939, the soldiers of the Red Army took their place, but by the end of the month they were forced to withdraw under the Molotov-Ribbentrop Pact, and the Germans returned to town. Many young Jews with the foresight to understand what was happening accompanied the

Soviet soldiers and headed east.

From the first days that the Germans entered, the town's Jews' had their rights revoked, their businesses confiscated, and they were forced to pay fines to the Germans. The Jews of the town were forbidden to come in contact with non-Jews, they were required to wear an identifying armband, and they were forbidden to walk on the sidewalks or be outside of their homes after six o'clock in the evening. The punishment for breaking the rules was death.

Towards the end of 1939, a *Judenrat* was established in the town and local Jews were later moved into a ghetto. With the expulsion of Jews from the surrounding villages, the Jewish population in town had grown to 3,300 people by May of 1940. In 1941, thousands more Jews were brought to the ghetto from nearby towns and villages and from Czechoslovakia.

Due to overcrowding, poor sanitary conditions and starvation, epidemics broke out in the ghetto. In October 1942, SS and German police along with Ukrainian police surrounded the ghetto. Jews were ordered to gather in the market square, where they were heavily guarded. While this was happening, their houses were searched and anyone found outside the square, especially the sick and the elderly, were shot on the spot. The Jews in the square were taken to the town's train station, and sent in cattle cars to the extermination camps at Sobibor and Belzec.

A short time before this *Aktion*, several Jewish families and young people escaped from the ghetto into the forests, where most of them joined partisan units. In the spring of 1943, a group of Jewish partisans organized under the command of Yehiel Greenspan, an Ostrow native who was mainly active in the Parczew forests.

It was only as they approached the town that Shurka asked her husband where they would live. She remembered the home of her aunt and uncle and hoped they might go there.

"Jews are only allowed to live inside the ghetto now."

"But you said that it is very crowded."

"Yes exactly, that's why several families have to squeeze in to one small apartment - sometimes six or seven people in the same room. Remember, my love," Avraham hugged her, "it is important to us to live with dignity even under these harsh conditions. We won't give up our values, habits or self-respect, because we are human beings."

"Mama taught me that I have to brush my teeth every morning, even back in the hut," said Irena.

"Very good."

"Also Alinka."

As they neared the ghetto, Avraham stopped.

"The yellow badge: don't forget that we have to wear it here."

In their small remote village, where only a few Jews lived, it had been easy to turn a blind eye to the decree. But here in the ghetto under Gestapo order they could not ignore the requirement to wear the star to identify themselves as Jews.

"It offends me," said Shurka as she was searching for the patch among her things, "that they mark us as if we were cows."

"It is not important. What is important is that in your heart you are human."

"And if I'm not..."

"What's gotten into you?" Avraham helped her put the badge on her arm. "It's nonsense, there's no need to be offended."

"But Avraham..."

"Keep your head up Shurka, be proud. Everyone should know who we are - proud Jews."

Little Irena looked at the band that her father tied tightly around the arm of her coat and did not say a word. Children understand that some things are better not to question.

At the entrance to the ghetto, flanked by barbed wire fences, Avraham presented his yellow badge and his work permit to the Polish guards, who let them enter. As they passed, one of the guards grabbed the doll that Irena held tightly in her hands, and his two friends burst out laughing.

"Mama... he took my... Alinka... Give her back... She's mine!" she shouted and tried to take the doll back. The guard lifted his rifle and aimed it at her. Avraham and Shurka froze on the spot.

Irena was silent. She stood before the Pole and held out her hands to him as though asking him to return her doll.

"It's a pretty doll," laughed the guard, "the doll of a princess. Isn't it a shame that she should live with dirty Jews?"

Avraham tried to pull Irena away but she insisted and kept standing before the Pole, her hands reaching out and hot tears streaming from her eyes. A German officer approached them and took the doll out of the guard's hands.

"That's my doll," insisted Irena and did not move from where she stood.

"You are a brave girl," he said to her and immediately added, "dirty Jew." He threw the doll on the ground. Irena bent to pick up her Alinka and Avraham held his breath. The Pole could very easily have pulled the trigger.

"Thank you," said Irena clutching the edge of her father's coat, from where she gave the officer a bashful smile to thank him.

The German gestured to them to keep moving.

Shurka felt her strength fail, and her legs could not carry her. She was about to faint. Avraham held her hand and pulled her along, silently thankful for their good luck. He knew that there had been a miracle; this incident could have ended very differently.

They stood at the gates of the ghetto. The sight was terrible.

The first thing that stunned Shurka as they entered the ghetto was the unbearable crowding. There was three times the usual number of the town's residents crammed together. Big carts, farmers' wagons and handcarts moved the property of the new residents who poured in, joining the masses against their will. In addition to the Jews of Ostrow, many refugees wound up in the ghetto. Reasonable apartments, accommodations that were barely decent enough to live in were snapped up quickly on a first-come-first-served basis.

A stench rose up from the sidewalks that Shurka did not remember from her previous visits; sewage flowed through the middle of the street. Peddlers crowded every corner trying to sell their belongings.

Old people in ragged clothes were begging. Shurka's gaze fell on the bickering women lined up for bread and the children digging through garbage bins, thin with hunger, their eyes expressionless.

The store owners no longer stood in the doorways of their businesses, selling house wares, shoes or colorful fabrics. The stores stood empty. Even the flower shop that had been across from the house she had lived in was closed. When people are hungry, flowers no longer move them.

Shurka soon learned from her husband the new reality into which she and her family had been cast.

"Before we go and meet your parents, I want you to understand the situation here and accept all of it."

"I smell it already," she tried to joke but Avraham was unsmiling.

"There is serious hunger in the Ostrow ghetto, much like in other ghettos. It is one of the German methods for annihilation - slower than the Zyklon, which they discovered later. The idea is to eliminate the Jews in the ghettos with a kind of 'natural death,' through methodical starvation. The Jews have been deprived of their food supplies, and their means of producing food, while traditional means of obtaining food - in exchange for money or trade, for example - have been forbidden."

"So where did you get the pear you gave to Irena?"

"We said not to ask, right? Listen, on top of everything, Jews have been forced to work - almost the whole population, ages 14 to 60. They don't even spare the elderly. The food rations for the forced laborers are portions fit for starving. People fight the increasing shortage of food through smuggling both publicly and privately. There is an organized smuggling network through the streets beside the fence, and there are agents and suppliers from the Polish population who have found a way to get rich by selling potatoes or eggs at exorbitant prices. The smuggled goods are divided among the food merchants in the ghetto. They need quick thinking and, above all, courage. They smuggle in sacks of flour, potatoes, fruits, milk and vegetables. Some of these items go to the public provisions organizations, to the communal kitchens and to other aid organizations."

"And you smuggle...?"

"Shurka, what did we say...?"

"God help us. What are they doing to us?" Shurka whispered.

"God is not watching over us anymore. Do you understand, woman? There is no Divine Providence in this place," Avraham replied.

"You can't speak that way," Shurka was shocked.

"God has abandoned us. It appears he went to look after the Germans, damn them, look around you." He hugged Shurka around her shoulders. "But we are still lucky. The ghetto is still open and it is possible to leave. They say that in Warsaw the situation is much worse... there you can't... but enough with these bad thoughts. Look who's coming..."

And the sorrow was immediately replaced with joy.

Coming toward them were Taiba and Yaakov Mendel and within moments they were hugging and laughing. Yaakov Mendel swung Irena onto his shoulders and Taiba carried quiet Yitzhak.

They hurried to the apartment that they had managed to secure. The tiny unit was in an old stone house, not far from the place where Uncle Yitzhak and his family used to live.

How far off those days seemed to Shurka now, when she had studied sewing, walked with her friends, made clothes of silk and velvet and spent her afternoon hours in their house playing with their children who adored her.

"This is our new palace, what do you say?" Yaakov Mendel tried to lighten the mood. Taiba explained proudly that only thanks to their good friends who knew important people in the ghetto where they able to get their hands on an apartment that would be big enough for all of them.

But Shurka saw the sorrow in her eyes and hugged her mother. Everything is alright. We are together. What else do we need?

Shurka and Irena looked around the place that Yaakov Mendel had called "our palace" but that was, in fact, a dim and neglected two-room apartment. There was no yard or flower garden and no blooming pear tree. There was no chest of drawers filled with Torah books and silverware. Only naked walls and a cracked floor. In the center of the room was a bucket to collect the water from the snow that leaked in from the roof. Beside the wall stood several simple wooden beds and beside them were big boxes that held all of their belongings. Shurka did not say a word. In times like these they had to be grateful for what they had. And here her wonderful family surrounded her like guardian angels.

Avraham and Shurka lived in the back room. Her parents and siblings, Ruska and Shlomo, crowded into the other room. They ate thin soup that Taiba managed to make from potatoes that her husband had obtained in some roundabout way. Sometimes Avraham would return from the work camp, which was still open and allowed him to leave and spend the night with his family now and then. From under his coat he would produce a cut of meat or a fishtail which he had miraculously procured from one of his Polish friends.

On their first night in the ghetto Yitzhak, as though protesting on behalf of the entire family, would not stop crying. His tiny body was hot. Shurka placed wet cloths on his forehead and tried to calm him. In the morning Dr. Davidowicz was rushed to him. He determined that the baby was sick with angina and needed medicine immediately or else, God forbid, he might get a lung infection in such a place as the ghetto.

Avraham returned from work pale and sweating with the medicine they needed in hand. Shurka did not ask and Avraham did not tell her where he had gotten it. She saw that the gold watch that her parents had given him for their wedding was no longer on his wrist. Avraham had also brought a little food, and even two candies for Irena. His talents in trade still served him well.

Every morning, new refugees arrived in the ghetto. Some

came by foot and some were brought by the Germans in trucks from which they were thrown into the streets with nobody to look out for them. Their faces were grim and they were curled up in their big coats with their children who had grown old before their time, trailing after them.

In apartments that had once held one family, three or four families were crammed. Due to the overcrowding, severe diseases broke out and a typhoid epidemic wreaked havoc among the residents. Wagons piled with corpses were an unforgettable sight.

Spring came to the Ostrow ghetto but the storks were not seen in the sky. People could come in and go out, though they were of course required to display the documents issued to them by the Germans.

Since the ghetto was still open, the two Yaakov Mendel managed to get occasional work on the surrounding farms. The farmers were happy to have skilled workers like them and their meager wages were enough to buy a bit of food for the family. Taiba and Shurka managed to prepare meals with the little that came in.

But if it seemed to them difficult to obtain food then, the worst was yet to come - the "Final Solution," declared at the Wannsee Conference, was just beginning.

One morning the family awoke to the sounds of knocking on their door. Nobody dared to move.

They had already learned that a knock on the door meant the worst. Expulsion.

But they heard a woman's voice.

"Jews, please, open up, take pity," they heard a woman's voice.

Yaakov Mendel hurried to the door. A young woman stood with a two-year-old girl in her arms. She did not wait for an invitation but burst in and sat down on the bench. The girl started to cry.

"Who are you?" Taiba hurried to her.

"Ella, this is my daughter Yelena. I have been banging on Jews' doors for an hour and nobody opened. Mercy, help me, we are hungry."

"Where are you from?" asked Taiba and served the shaking woman a dish of potato soup. She brought the little girl some milk.

"From the Lubartow ghetto - I had to escape. Yesterday they started to transfer some of the ghetto residents to the Sobibor. Have you heard about Sobibor?"

Yaakov Mendel signaled to Shurka and she went to the other room to protect little Irena from the things Ella was saying.

"We heard that it is a newer work camp."

"Don't believe what they are saying. They are murdering Jews."

"Who said that?"

"My younger sister managed to escape from there. She worked in the camp clearing out the bodies. She told me what happens there, about the crematoria, the showers. Horrors not even the devil could have imagined. "

"Do you know anyone from Ostrow who could help you?"

"Not a living soul. My husband was sent to a work camp far away and we remained, just the two of us, alone in the world. Give me a place to rest my head for just a few days. After that I am moving to the forest. That's why I came here, it is close to the Parczew Forest."

"What is in the forest?"

"You didn't hear? Yehiel Greenspan started a fighters' camp."

"What about the child?"

"We will live in the nearby family camp."

Taiba looked at her husband. For some days now she had been telling him that they could not stay here. That Ostrow was a trap. That there were rumors of new decrees and Aktions, of whole families stabbed in the middle of the night in order to make room for others.

Ella lived in their house for three days. On the fourth she bade them farewell.

A brother of a friend of the family, a Polish farmer, picked her up from the ghetto entrance and took her to the forest.

"Don't wait. Come and join us," she told them before she departed. "This ghetto will be destroyed and then what?"

"As long as Yitzhak can't travel we aren't going anywhere," Yaakov Mendel replied.

"And what about the others?"

"They will wait. It's just a matter of a few months... nothing will happen."

"All we need is to know is where we are getting the next potato."

14.

In July, the ghetto awoke to a new level of horror.

The Aktions began. "Aktion" refers to the "operation" whereby the Gestapo grouped Jews together in the ghettos for deportation to the concentration camps, extermination camps, or forced labor camps. Jewish families disappeared in the middle of night until the ghetto was completely emptied.

The Germans had now moved onto the last phase of the Final Solution of Europe's Jews and they had begun to systematically thin out the population. The ghetto transformed from a residential environment to a death trap for the many Jews crowded there, and as a transfer station to the concentration camps.

July was at the beginning of their fifth month of living in the ghetto.

The signs began to appear.

In the middle of the night, the family awoke to the clamor of German boots on the pavement.

They stayed in their beds. It was clear that nothing good would come of this night visit. The steps passed by their house. They wondered where the Germans were headed, and for whom they were looking. Afterward they heard the screams of children, the weeping of women who had been torn from their loved ones, the sound of shots ringing out. When silence returned to the street again, nobody dared to move. It was better to wait for morning.

"Bad news awaits," said Taiba as she pulled Yitzhak to her.

Uncle Yodel (Yehuda) who had joined them in the ghetto a little after their arrival, came to their house at the crack of dawn and told them that that night the Germans had rounded up about one hundred people and sent them on trucks to an improved labor camp at Treblinka.

"Like Sobibor?" asked Yaakov Mendel.

"Terrible like Sobibor," said Yodel. "There are those who think they are lucky to be sent away from here, that anything would be better than the ghetto. No one could imagine the fate awaiting the women, children and elderly people they took."

"But maybe it really is an improved camp," said Aunt Alinka. "With fresh air and healthy food."

"Nonsense, I am telling you that this nighttime business is a general rehearsal for the dissolution of the ghetto."

"He's right," Shurka said, "Hitler never hid his intentions."

"... to exterminate the entire Jewish people."

In August, news began to arrive about what was happening in the concentration camps. Indeed, these were not labor camps or new settlements but places whose residents were condemned to death.

"It's just like Ella told us,"

"She...?"

"To the forest."

"And what about you?"

"We have to get out of here. Why should you wait...?"

When the rumors persisted, the family and other relatives planned to leave the ghetto and head to the woods.

They knew that in the great Parczew Forest, the edge of which could be seen on the way to the city, many Jews who refused to stay in the ghettos were in hiding.

They had to hurry. If they were to have a hope of surviving the war they had to take advantage of this narrow window of opportunity and escape while the ghetto gates were still open.

They hoped that there, in the forest, they would feel safe, that they would be well hidden from the Germans and the Polish collaborators.

"Look what has happened," said Shurka, "Poland has no place for Jews. The forest is our last place of refuge."

15.

It was not an easy decision to leave the ghetto and head for the forest. There were bitter arguments within the Shidlovsky household... to stay and hope that the war would end soon and that life would return to the way it was or to take a huge risk and go out into the unknown? And if they were to go, where to? To Russia or to the forests?

Avraham was fixed in his belief that the only possible refuge was the forest. Shurka and her parents agreed with him.

Others argued with him that maybe it would be better to wait for the next deportation and see what was really happening.

If they fled to the forest they would be exposed to natural disasters and human cruelty. Nature's risks included rain, snow, wind and cold, illness, hunger and scarcity. Since they had no food, no medicine, no weapons, how could they survive such conditions? But the greater dangers were gangs of looters and murderers, poor peasant farmers that would inform on Jews, and Germans who from time to time went to hunt those who had gone into hiding...

The goal of the Jewish partisans who fled to the forests was not limited to their own survival.

These young warriors protected Jews who had no weapons, women and children who hid in the forest. They procured food from the farmers through theft or force. They took it upon themselves to punish those peasants who had turned in

Jews. But their ultimate goal was to procure weapons. Without a weapon one was helpless. They led operations in order to get their hands on weapons.

Each possibility came with enormous risks, especially as Devorah was pregnant and Avraham and Shurka had young children.

On the one hand there were rumors that the Germans planned to move the population in order to settle them in a new place in the east, that they had built more comfortable work camps to settle the Jews, that the meaning of the "Final Solution" was simply to resettle the Jews. On the other hand there were those who argued that it was a plan for extermination. That the Germans were not to be trusted.

"Maybe we will wait and see what really happens? You know, every Jew has a different opinion and there are more rumors than rats," Yaakov Mendel said to his son-in-law.

"Exactly. Who knows that we won't be 'out of the frying pan and into the fire?'" agreed the uncle.

"What do you suggest?" Avraham was indignant, "that we wait for the next Aktion? Until they put us on the trains? I don't understand you - we must act, not wait!" He spoke passionately, confidently claiming that now, while the ghetto gates were still open, there was still a chance, maybe a last chance.

Everyone gathered around him, tense and listening. His confidence drew others to him. Shurka said a silent prayer that they would know the right decision to make. She worried about the fate of her children. Irena was barely four years old and Yitzhak was still weak - in uncertain conditions he might get sick again and in the forest it would be hard to take proper care of him.

"The Jews in the forest are also at risk," Yaakov Mendel

wavered. "It is known that the partisans belonging to the Home Army battalions are looking for an opportunity not only to do damage to the Germans but also to exterminate the Jews. Whoever is caught in the forest will be handed over."

"And what choice do we have? To go like sheep to the slaughter?"

The room fell silent. Only the sound of little Yitzhak crying was heard. Shurka bit her lip. She did not ask what would become of her son in the forest. She trusted her husband.

Avraham had made up his mind. He heard what was reported by refugees who had managed to jump off the trains. They spoke of the inhuman conditions of the journey, and of terrible places like Treblinka and Sobibor. He knew much more than he could tell his family. He had no doubt in his mind that the ghetto would not be safe any longer and that there was no choice but to go to the forest and try to join the communist partisans.

"The Ludowa Army operates in the Parczew Forest," he said. "There are Polish and Russian partisans living peacefully together with Jews."

"The Poles turn in Jews and chase them. We don't need to get mixed up with them," argued Yosef, Taiba's younger brother.

But Avraham explained, "I am speaking about the Ludowa Army. They take Jews into their service. They are armed. Yehiel Greenspan and his soldiers joined them. Instead of waiting in fear, they attack military convoys, raid the homes of collaborators and blow up railroad tracks. They live with dignity and don't sit idle." He looked around at the family, gathered up Irena and said, "The decision is in your hands. Whatever we do, we will do it as one united family."

Yaakov Mendel put his arm around Taiba and said that he supported Avraham. It was better to act and not wait.

"And what does one live on in the forest - heroes also need food, no?" argued Taiba.

"I heard that the peasants are afraid of them and provide them with food. If not, they take it by force."

"And what will we do when the winter comes?"

"We will find a solution by then. Maybe the war will be over by winter and we can go home."

"Living in the forest is a solution?" Aunt Rachel wrung her hands. "I have seven children. I am afraid of those forests - they could be a death trap."

"What do you suggest?" her husband Yehuda asked her.

"To stay, not to take the risk. Who said that they will throw everyone out?" she answered.

"And the ghetto? You live here and you know about the Aktions. Here, two days ago in the street next to ours they took six families in the middle of the night..."

"Until now we have managed."

"You remind me of the children of Israel who wanted to return to Pharaoh. We have to leave - not to fear the possibility of freedom."

"Enough, enough!" Shurka quieted them. "We decided not to separate, so any decision we make will be all of ours. Tell me," she turned to her husband, "are you sure that the partisans in the forests will agree to accept women and small children?"

"I suggest that we head there and try to get organized by ourselves. We will live as one big family."

"Alone? Just us? It would be better to get together with a larger community."

"Slowly, slowly we will organize ourselves. There are already dozens of families there. Every day more and more people flee to the forest. For now it is still possible and we cannot miss this window of opportunity."

"We can't stay," Yaakov Mendel joined his son-in-law's argument. "The forest will be a kind of defensive wall for us. The Germans are afraid of the big swamps so they don't send forces in there. Avraham is right, living here might look easier but the ghetto will soon be cleared out."

The arguments went on for days until something happened that made Shurka decide to leave once and for all.

One morning she took Irena and the two went to the meager market where one could still get potatoes and cabbage for soup. On the way she stumbled over someone on the sidewalk and she and Irena fell on top of him. She realized immediately that they had fallen on a dead man.

There were flies buzzing around him. His hand still held a box in which he had hoped to receive some handout, perhaps a piece of bread that would save him from his desperate hunger.

"Mama look, a box, should we take it?" Irena asked and opened the dead man's box. Shurka regained her composure, got up quickly, gathering up the little girl before she understood, trying to spare her the terrible sight. She summoned the burial society and hurried away. When she returned to the house she had made up her mind.

"We have to get out of this place where you can't even die with dignity." That night they all reached agreement.

They had to leave quickly - in the great forests of Parczew they might have a chance of surviving the war.

"Just for a few months," Avraham, optimistic as always, said to Shurka and the rest of the family.

"How do you know?"

"Enough. We must trust in God."

"You said he is no longer looking over us."

"We have a new God now and he is in the forest. Start packing."

"Tell me about Yehiel Greenspan and the new God in the forest."

And Avraham told her about the Jewish hero and the place where Jews took their fate into their own hands.

"In the Parczew Forest, which you know from fairy tales, the Jewish partisans set up two camps: one for partisan warriors, and another, the 'family camp,' which is a refuge for women, children and the elderly. The family camp is called 'Tabur' (and also 'Bazar'). The partisan force protects the family camp."

"And where will you live?"

"Don't worry about that, Wife. Your hiding place is my hiding place, your refuge is my refuge. The most important Jewish partisan unit in Poland operates in the Parczew Forest; the one commanded by Yehiel Greenspan."

"My sister Ruska wants to join the fighters."

"They will be happy to have her. The Jewish partisans also have women who participate in the battles - as fighters with weapons, or as medics."

In addition to Avraham and Shurka's small family, the group setting off to the forests included Yaakov Mendel and Taiba, Ruska and Shlomo, Devorah and her husband, Yodel and his wife Rachel and their seven children. Ruska did not stay with them but served in the fighters' camp, at first as a medic and later as a fighter.

To the Forests

Now that the decision had been made, difficult questions arose as to where exactly would they go - the forest was enormous.

Would they find their acquaintances in the forest?

Would they have to live alone? To seek out the partisans? Would the partisans be willing to accept two families with so many small children, the baby, and Devorah who soon would no longer be able to hide her pregnancy? How would they survive the harsh winter months? Would they manage to find food?

It was concluded that Avraham and Yaakov Mendel would head out first to the forests, try to make contact with those hiding there and hear from them about the details of life in the wild. This way they could better plan the escape by learning what to bring, and how to plan the route.

Ten days later, Yaakov Mendel and Avraham returned. Their faces were flushed with happiness. Everything was ready. The time had come.

In order not to endanger themselves, it was decided that each family would go out on its own. They set up a place where they could rendezvous in the forest.

Avraham made them a precise map with a designated meeting place. Afterwards, they decided, they would go together to find the family camp. The first thing was to find shelter in the forest...

August 1942. There were already light winds and signs of autumn in the air; the nights were cold and the leaves began to fall. This was the month that both families would set off toward the forest.

And how could they have known that in September of that same year, only one month later, all the Jews in the ghetto would be sent to Treblinka and murdered?

Ostrow Lubelski, like other cities in Poland - Lubartow, Parczew and Lublin - were places where Jews and Poles would never again live side by side. Their hundred-year-old harmony had been brutally interrupted, sweeping away a community of millions of people.

By the time the ghetto was evacuated in September 1942, Shurka and her family were already experienced forest dwellers. First they had found a place to hide themselves and later they had joined the family camp.

Soon they would become part of Yehiel Greenspan's band of forest dwellers. The forest would be their living space and the people would be their protective wall. But more people perished in the forest than survived. For many, the forest was their final resting place.

The Partisans in the Forests of Poland

One of the ways that Jews protected themselves against the Nazis in occupied Europe was to flee the crowded ghettos to partisan camps established in the big forests among the mountains and swamplands - areas that the organized army would have difficulty reaching.

The journey from the ghetto to the forests was dangerous and the chances of reaching the partisan units were slim. Escapees were forced to pass through hostile villages and settlements and risk being spotted and turned in by informants.

So as not to leave their families behind in the ghetto, the Jewish partisans brought their families along. This made operating in the forests that much harder as they had constantly to worry about the families' wellbeing and to provide enough food. For this purpose, "family camps" were established that functioned as small independent units. The known family camps included the Bielski camp in Belarus and Yehiel Greenspan's camp in the Parczew Forest, where Shurka and her family went to hide.

But the forests were not a safe place for Jews either. People from the Krayova Army were extreme anti-Semites and even murdered Jews who fled to the forests. From the spring of 1942 onward, there were "wild" gangs and groups of partisans operating in the forest whose primary goal was to catch Jews.

The Germans did not stop searching for Jews who had escaped to the forest. They were helped by Poles. During Christmas of 1942, Passover of 1943 and in May of 1944, the Germans organized large hunts in the Parczew Forest, during which they murdered most of the people hiding (over 4,000 people). However, the family camp was not entirely destroyed and Yehiel Greenspan's unit mostly survived.

16.

They left the ghetto in the middle of the night. It was dark outside. Although it was still summer, the sky was covered by heavy clouds as though a heavy rain might fall at any moment. Only the lights of houses in the village glittered in the distance and dotted the mountains with pale points of light.

The world was still asleep.

The little children slept too.

They wrapped Irena in a big wool blanket, rolling her as though she were a package. She wore a black knit hat that covered her face and her shoes were tied with a rope so that they would not fall off. One could not live in the forest without shoes.

Shurka sat in the wagon, holding little Yitzhak tightly in her arms. Avraham covered the three of them with a big blanket.

Devorah, whose pregnancy was not yet showing, walked alongside the men who pulled the wagon after them. They had built it by hand throughout the previous month from scraps they had found - pieces of wood and rickety wheels. They loaded it with the equipment they had managed to acquire and that was absolutely necessary. Blankets, coats, clothes, food for a few days and cooking utensils - everything that Avraham instructed them to bring.

"Click-clack," the wooden wheels thumped as they bounced over the stones of the ghetto street.

"Click-clack," answered the sounds of their steps.

The wind whistled in their ears and sometimes they heard the cry of a raven or dogs barking. Sometimes shots rang out in the quiet night but they kept moving and did not stop.

Another moment and they stood by the eastern gate. Nobody spoke. They knew just one thing - they had to manage to get to the meeting point at the edge of the forest before sunrise.

Quietly they passed by the Polish guard sleeping in his little hut, his eyes closed and head slumped on the back of the chair. An empty bottle of vodka stood beside him. Maybe, Shurka would consider later, her husband and father had wisely paid him in advance with a bottle of vodka. In any case, he was so drunk that he did not notice the handful of people leaving under the cover of darkness.

They passed through the first gate, then the second. One more moment - their hearts were pounding. And then they were outside. They hurried on and a moment later the city disappeared.

They headed east toward the big forest.

They walked for four hours, dragging the cart which carried Shurka and the children. Every now and then she would set Irena and Yitzhak down on their pillow, cover them and get out to help pull.

Avraham, who knew the way well, headed the procession.

Shurka was proud of her husband. Taller than everyone, with his eyes burning, he led them to freedom.

After the night, the pale first rays of light caressed their cheeks like a promise of better days to come. The ghetto slipped farther behind in the distance, along with its strong smells and harsh sights.

When morning came and the sun drove the clouds away, Irena awoke. She sat up in the cart, looked around and burst into tears. Shurka hurried to her. She hugged her daughter and asked that they stop so she could explain where they were going.

"Impossible," said Avraham, and urged them to move forward.

"But she—"

"There's no way we can do that. Calm her quickly before one of the good-hearted Poles wakes up."

He worried about being seen by the Polish villagers along their way. These days it was hard to tell a good man from a collaborator.

Shurka placed Alinka doll in Irena's hands and suggested she hum her a song. Shurka pointed to the trees along their way and taught Irena their names...

"This is the oak, this is the elm, there you will see the pines, and the little bushes are raspberry and blueberry."

Yitzhak lay dozing in the wagon. Every now and then he opened his black eyes and looked at the sky.

"That child is too quiet," thought Taiba, "he worries me," but she kept her concern to herself.

When they got to a small grove, not far from the big swamp, Avraham stopped and signaled to them to stay quiet. In the stillness around them they heard the wind blowing through the treetops, the chirping of the songbirds that had just woken with the first light and the buzz of the immense mosquitos that seemed to rejoice at the arrival of newcomers.

"What now?" whispered Shurka. "Do you know which way we need to turn?"

"Wait for me here. And it is very important that you do your best to stay quiet."

"Where, Avraham?" Shurka worried.

"To the meeting point with the guides."

"Who are they?"

"They know every corner of the forest and they are waiting

for us and will show us a place where we can set up our forest home. Wait and don't worry."

Avraham disappeared out of sight.

One moment passed and then another. They huddled close together. They heard a whistle followed by another and then hushed voices.

A short while later, which felt like an eternity, Avraham returned accompanied by two young men in army boots and heavy woolen coats. Their glance lingered on Irena and they whispered something to Avraham.

"Don't worry."

"They are so little."

"The children will be okay," Avraham promised them.

"I don't know," the taller of the two hesitated. "The forest can be a brutal place for children."

"They have already gone through one journey. They survived the ghetto - they are strong and smart and they know what is required of them in times of danger."

"I hope you're right," said the tall one. He approached Irena who was clutching Shurka, handed her a red apple and said, "I'm David and that that is my brother Shlomo."

"I am Irena and this is Alinka."

"Nice to meet you. Your father says we can count on you. Is he right?"

"My father knows best. I am not even afraid of wolves. If they come, my father will beat them," Irena answered and everyone burst out laughing.

For a moment, the tension abated.

"Shlomo and David? Who are they? I have never seen them before," Taiba whispered to her husband.

Yaakov Mendel signaled to her with his fingers that it was

forbidden to speak or ask questions. David and Shlomo instructed them to follow after them, deep into the forest.

They trudged behind them to a place where people who were unfamiliar were afraid to go, past the big swamps that were supposed to protect them.

The forest was loud. There was always a murmur, like the echo of distant bells, a hazy memory from other times. They went deeper, now and then having to go around puddles that had collected from the summer rains. They avoided the swamps. This was the complex inner part of the ancient forest, which had not yet seen a saw or an ax.

Shurka tried to understand where they were. She raised her head but the tall treetops blocked the sky: mighty oaks, broad elms, white-trunked birches and hundred-year-old pines. The forest was dark. Lone rays of sunlight managed to penetrate the thick canopy.

Bright ferns sprouted through the carpet of pine needles that covered the forest floor like soft muslin. In the damp crooks grew green brush, blackberry bushes and purple blueberries that perfumed the air and over everything was the sound of the forest. That constant murmur would accompany them in the coming days.

"Listen," Irena said to Shurka. "The trees are groaning."

"They are happy to see us," Shurka assured her.

"These old trees have seen everything," said Avraham. "But they haven't seen such people as this, ragged and miserable, coming to hide themselves and make the forest their home."

The two guides told them to be quiet. To move forward.

When they got to a little clearing in the forest, the two stopped, waved to Yaakov Mendel and Avraham and promptly disappeared.

"Where did they—?" the question rose on Shurka's lips but her husband's expression silenced her.

"What do we do now?" asked Taiba. "The children are hungry already."

"We're here... this is the place," said Avraham. Then he raised his eyes to the sky.

"A new day, a new life. May it be good to the Jews! It's time for breakfast."

"Already? I thought we were joining other families that live in the forest."

"This is the place. Many families are scattered throughout the forest, each on their own. In the meantime we will live here. It is dangerous to group together and attract the Poles and the Germans. This place suits us, at least as a beginning."

"I don't understand. Where are the others?"

"I told you, they are all over the forest. Each family has found its own place, one that suits them."

"And when will we meet up with them?" asked Shurka. She was disappointed. She had imagined them all living together and building a new community, looking after one another and the children making friends.

"The others? What about the others?"

"First of all we must organize our place for ourselves, then we will see. Eventually we will adapt to the forest and then we can look for the others."

"I thought—"

"Please," Avraham said. "Trust me."

"I don't understand," Taiba insisted. "There is no house here, not even a hut. Where will we live?"

Avraham smiled broadly.

"Here we will build our new house. This is the place."

"House?" marveled Shurka, "In the forest? What are you talking about? Where are there houses here? Why not join the others?" She still hoped that life in the family camp would be more comfortable.

"There are houses, but they are underground."

"Underground?"

"I never heard of a house like that," Irena laughed.

"Exactly. They're called bunkers - the earth here is soft and there are many bushes around that we can use to cover the opening." He hugged her. "Our bunker will be our fortress, our home that we will build with our own hands."

"We will live underground?"

"Like ants?" exclaimed Irena with delight. She was happy in the forest. She liked smelling the leaves and scattering the pine needles.

"More or less. Don't worry, our security is the top priority."

The family members appeared perplexed and doubtful. This is what he had planned for them? To live underground in a bunker? Were they mistaken when they had assumed that the forest would be more comfortable?

"Avraham, maybe we should go back."

"Where?"

"To the ghetto."

"No."

"He's right," said Yaakov Mendel. "Wait and see, we will build the most comfortable, most beautiful bunker in the world."

They spent their first night and many others on a bed of leaves in a clearing in the forest. The weather was pleasant and comfortable.

All of the family members helped build the bunker, each according to his or her ability. The men dug up the earth with tools that they had brought with them, and the women cleared the dirt that had been dug up and scattered it in the forest to hide any evidence from suspicious eyes. Even Irena helped her father. With her little hands she scratched at the earth and scattered it around. They lined the floor of the bunker with moss and supported the walls with strong branches.

On the fifth day, their hiding place was ready.

"The first night in our dugout bunker was a nightmare," Shurka later told her grandchildren and showed them the drawings that Irena had made. "It was hard for me to sleep... my body was restless. It was as though the earth beneath me was moving, and every noise made me jump. I heard the howling of wolves and the whistling of the wind from afar, but above all it was little Yitzhak that I was worried about. All of us worried. He looked weak and pale, and when I gave him a cloth dipped in milk to suck on, he looked at me with sad eyes and turned his head. Sometimes he would let out a little whimper, as though telling me how hard it was for him, how weak he was; it broke my heart."

They began their lives as forest people. The bunker was too small and crowded. It was hard for them to sleep there. Nights became cold and days grew short.

Slowly they grew accustomed to the difficult reality. After coming to terms with the new circumstances, Shurka and Taiba went out to collect wood for the fire so that they could cook the potatoes and cabbage they had brought with them. From time to time they met other women who lived in the forest.

Irena ran around constantly, collecting acorns and playing with pine needles. Shurka looked after Yitzhak, trying to encourage him, to make him laugh. Taiba searched for berries and edible plants. Avraham would disappear for a few hours at a time and return with some vegetables and a loaf of bread. Yaakov Mendel tried to clean, organize, improve on and expand the bunker a little every day.

Taiba urged him to try to find relatives or acquaintances who she knew were also hiding in the forest, but he was not willing to leave his family.

"Everyone has a role here," he told her. "Avraham, 'Mister Plenty' is the Minister of Supplies and I am the Minister of the Interior."

"And I am the Minister of Cooking," laughed Taiba.

"And what am I?" asked Irena.

"You are the princess of the forest."

The second week, another family joined them. The Kofit family, like them, had come from Ostrow Lubelski and had fled to the forest.

"What's new in Ostrow?" asked Shurka, hoping to hear that maybe they had been worrying for naught, that perhaps they could go back.

"It gets worse every day."

"It was already bad."

"The situation is more terrible all the time. There are Aktions, they say they want to clear out the ghetto."

"Do you know where the Jews have been taken?"

"Nobody who was taken has ever returned. They say that—" Leah Kofit spoke but Avraham hurried to quiet her. Irena did not miss a word.

Yaakov Mendel and Avraham were happy about the new people. It was nicer when there was another family and friends to speak with. There were children to play with Irena and they helped them to build a bunker not far from their own. They already had the skills and experience.

"My Saba builds the best bunkers in the world," Irena said proudly.

"And what about me?" asked Taiba.

"You make the best soup in the whole forest."

A month passed, and still they crowded into the bunker all together every night, the Shidlovsky's in their bunker and the Kofit's in their own.

"That phase was the hardest," Shurka would smile as she told her grandchildren, years later.

"A different life, everyone just looked out for himself. We were like little tribes scattered throughout the forests. The others were like shadows passing beside us in the night. Sometimes we met acquaintances. Each family had its own story and its own way of surviving. We tried to encourage one another. At the end of September we heard rumors that the ghetto had been liquidated once and for all and that all of its inhabitants had been sent to concentration camps. We felt that maybe we were lucky. A few weeks more passed and we had practically forgotten our previous lives - it seemed as though we had always lived like this.

"Humans can adapt to anything. The truth is, our survival was in no small part due to my Avraham, Mister Plenty, who managed to get us bread and vegetables somehow. And I never asked how."

Autumn gave way to winter. The days grew shorter and strong winds blew. Soon the days of snow and real cold would come.

One morning several men dressed in soldiers' uniforms stopped beside their camp. They called to Avraham and Yaakov

Mendel. When the two returned, their faces were joyful.

"We're leaving!" called out Avraham, "Let's go."

"Where to now?"

"Not far from here, they invited us to join the family camp, we will be together, just like you wanted. Come on, we have to get going. They are waiting for us there."

"And our bunker?"

"It will remain here. Who knows... maybe someday we will need it."

"We will have two forest homes!" said Shurka happily.

"Do you think that the camp will be better than what we have here?"

"I know it will. They set up an organized, safe family camp, right beside the warriors' camp. We will be part of one big family - the partisans of Yehiel Greenspan."

They quickly packed up their belongings, folded the blankets, gathered up their few tools and clothes and continued to the new meeting place, the camp.

Even before they saw the others, the smell of stew and campfire reached their noses. As they approached they heard people's hushed voices, and when they emerged from the forest, they saw them - sitting around the campfire, polishing weapons, dressing wounds and engaged in various crafts like busy ants. Everything was done silently. Nobody dared to raise his voice or laugh.

Upon seeing the small group approaching, they stopped their tasks and gathered to look at them. For a moment they stared, fearful that the newcomers had been followed by Jew-hunters.

"Look, there are the two Yaakov Mendels," one of them cried, and another whispered, "Welcome, Jews!" And they immediately hurried to them with tears of joy. Everyone was chattering and asking, hoping they had some news about relatives who had stayed behind.

"We heard they've cleared out the Ostrow ghetto."

"All the Jews got onto the trains."

"Do you understand the meaning of those trains? It's not a trip to freedom, it's a death march."

One bright-eyed woman served bowls of soup to revive them.

"Eat, eat," she urged them. "This is our royal feast," another laughed. "We make soup from whatever we can find. Better you don't ask what's inside besides potatoes and barley."

Taiba tasted it and said that she had not had such good soup in years, "And I don't care what's inside."

After the initial meeting, the family began to get organized. Their relatives planned to arrive the following day and they had to hurry to build themselves a new house. The camp commander, a ruddy young man with a dirty bandage covering his forehead, showed them where their future bunker would be built.

"The earth here is soft and nice," he said, "and all of us are here to help."

And indeed, the camp veterans were happy to help them. Shovels and hoes were passed from hand to hand and bags filled with stones and support beams were piled around them. The soft earth made it easy for them to dig. Just a few hours later a big pit had been dug.

While their bunker was not yet completed, they were hosted in the "bunker palaces" of other families, who had made space for them and shared their bedding. A few days later their bunker was ready. It was wide and comfortable from the beginning.

Then they had to divide the space wisely among the growing

family: Yehuda, his wife Rachel and their seven children, several cousins who had managed to leave the ghetto in time, Taiba and Yaakov Mendel, Devorah and her husband Shamai, Shlomo the youngest, and of course Shurka, Avraham, Irena and Yitzhak. It was not simple. One family, one bunker, many tensions. Each of them tried to get a softer part of the bunker, close to the entrance where the air was fresher.

Avraham tried to make their move into a celebration, to make Irena laugh, to make little Yitzhak happy. He scattered salt around the big pit for good luck and asked everyone to pray together to the Master of the Universe to protect them.

"Though I walk through the valley of the shadow of death, I will fear no evil," he read aloud and all the people around him wiped away a tear.

"Have you rediscovered God?" Shurka asked him.

"He found me," he embraced her.

Now they had their own home. The bunker was dug well and its roof was veiled with plants and shrubs. Yaakov Mendel stood beside the big pit and helped Taiba down. Afterwards he waved at Irena and helped her down too. Then Shurka and Avraham descended, followed by the rest of the family. They unpacked the bundles they had brought and organized their new home.

They lived in their hiding place for several months before they were forced to move even deeper into the forest and build a new bunker.

Whenever the Germans raided the forest, they were forced to start over.

"Instead of cleaning, we move houses," said Yaakov Mendel and everyone laughed wryly.

17.

Irena quickly adapted to the changes and found there were advantages to their new life in the woods.

She loved the forest and would play between the bunkers, gathering leaves, collecting smooth rocks and helping out in the kitchen. She picked berries, discovered mushrooms and learned the songs of the birds. Thanks to her joyous laugh and vitality, she soon became well-loved around the camp.

She got used to not complaining: neither about the food, the conditions, nor the crowding. Even if two days passed without a bowl of hot soup, she learned to find a filling meal among the forest fruits and berries.

Shurka observed her little Irena playing among the fighters and learning from them how to whistle through leaves and names of trees, and she prayed that someday she would be able to give her little girl back what had been taken from her... Home.

"Do you miss our house?" Shurka once asked her, unable to restrain herself.

The girl stared at her mother with the look of a child who has grown up before her time and said: "My home is wherever you are Mama. We will stay together, right?"

Baby Yitzhak, on the other hand, was struggling and growing weaker. Shurka would hold him to her heart, sing to him, shower him with love and pray to the God of Abraham and

Yaakov to give him strength to survive the forest. She no longer had milk for him and he refused to eat the thin soup that she spooned into his mouth.

Shurka tried everything, wetting his lips and begging him to suck on the cloth dipped in soup because who knew what tomorrow would bring. And Yitzhak? He would suck and fall asleep instantly, as though his strength had failed him. From time to time the fighters would return from a raid in the nearby villages and bring her milk that Taiba would heat up for him, but he would not drink and had even stopped smiling.

Soon the daily life of the family camp became routine.

They grew accustomed to being very quiet during the day-time, so as not to, God forbid, draw any attention. They stayed inside the bunkers as much as possible and tried to keep away from the center of the camp.

Everybody had a role in the family camp. Each family was responsible for cleaning its own bunker as well as fixing and improving it. They had to bury their waste so as not to attract wolves or rats. There were those whose role was to guard or to be in contact with the fighters' camp but Avraham had a special role. Early in the morning he would go out on his missions.

"Where are you hurrying off to?" Shurka would ask her husband. "It's still dark outside."

"I'm with the supply force," he would declare half-joking, half-serious, "not for nothing they call me 'Mister Plenty.'"

Only during the evening hours did the camp residents group together, cooking and chatting and living a communal life. Some evenings Avraham too would return.

Shurka would spot a cut of sausage inside his coat and carrots under his wool scarf from which she would make soup to warm them up, and she never asked a thing. Indeed, he always cautioned her not to.

In addition to Irena, there were two other children in the camp who were a little older. When darkness would fall, Haim the teacher would gather them and tell stories from the Torah, about the fathers and the mothers: Yosef who went down to Egypt and Noah who built the ark. He even had a book of fairy tales from which he read to them.

"Avraham," Shurka once requested, "when you go on your mission that I am forbidden to ask about, maybe look for a children's book."

And Mr. Plenty indeed found one.

Gradually, the family camp began to feel like an organized settlement.

During the morning hours the camp residents would go out through the pit opening, stretch their limbs and clean up their shelter. They would air out the blankets, pile up the laundry, stamp down the earth and refresh the branches that camouflaged the bunker rooftops.

Breakfast was a slice of bread and a little weak tea. Everybody was instructed to do his part for the common good. The cooks cooked, the carpenters helped prepare supports for the bunkers and built temporary furniture that they could take apart immediately, the tailors made a great effort to patch the heavy coats where holes gaped, but most important of all, the shoemakers had their hands full with work. They had to constantly invent new ways to mend all the worn out shoes.

The fighters would bring raw materials to the camp that they had seized from the villages so that a new heel could be fashioned from wood, or a hole patched in a sole.

The welders and the blacksmiths were busy repairing weapons to return them to action. Even the barbers had work to do.

The fighters and even the Russian partisans would come to the camp for a decent haircut.

When new additions joined the family camp, each person was asked what they could contribute.

"I'm a seamstress," said Shurka, and immediately joined the team of tailors and seamstresses. Rachel was with the gatherers and Yaakov Mendel joined the carpenters.

Shurka worked to patch, shorten and mend whatever was needed. Every scrap of fabric was used to the fullest. They took apart old coats that the partisans had managed to obtain and Shurka used the pieces to refashion coats for women and children.

Taiba was part of the kitchen team where, with the help of much imagination and meager ingredients, they worked to prepare meals for the dozens of people. Even Shurka, to whom it seemed that life in the camp was especially difficult, took on a role in the kitchen.

Little Irena also joined the team. She used the daylight hours for her forest adventures, though never far from the eyes and supervision of the guards. In time, it became a very useful activity, when she would bring back berries that she found in the bushes.

Eventually Shurka understood what her husband did and how he managed to bring some vegetables, eggs or even the occasional sausage back to camp. The men with families who were not considered fighters were responsible for supplies.

They went out to the nearby farms in order to get food in whatever way they could - paying, begging, sometimes taking, and sometimes - if there was no other choice - by force.

Their mission was very dangerous because there could be informants among the peasant farmers or plotting among other partisans who roamed the forest and searched for weapons.

"What happened to you today?"

"Today? A sharp-eyed peasant woman saw me and started shouting and nearly alarmed the entire German army."

"What did you do?"

"What can you do?"

"The truth," Shurka revealed once, "is it's hard to know who we must fear more: the Germans, the Poles, or the other partisans. But most of all, the Polish army."

18.

And while the summer passed in relative calm, pleasant and cool, the threat of winter made everyone worry. That year's autumn had been particularly harsh. The snow came early and already by the first of December the forest was covered with a white blanket and a bitter cold descended on Poland. Conditions in the forest became harsh. It was no longer possible to find the berries or mushrooms to supplement their diet and people went about the camp both hungry and wrapped in blankets, their hands covered with whatever scraps of fabric they could find. Shoes got wet and began to crack and David Hanan, the shoemaker, was constantly forced to reinvent ways to mend them.

"I have become a medic, not a shoemaker," he smiled and bandaged the sole of a shoe or tied ragged leather bits together with a dirty bandage.

The winter also brought new trouble: the Germans.

They had heard of Jews hiding out of reach in the Parczew Forest and this news made them very angry. Up to that point they had avoided entering the forest, wary of the big swamps which only those who knew the terrain well could safely avoid.

What the Jews feared indeed happened. The Germans found people to help them. The villagers who suffered from the partisan raids informed on them and for a few pennies or maybe a bottle of vodka they agreed to serve as guides to the Germans.

The heavy snow aided their search, making footprints easily recognizable. So the Jewish camp residents received a new instruction: if there was a warning from the guards about a planned raid, it was absolutely forbidden to flee. They would have to regroup, descend immediately into the bunkers and remain completely silent.

"What do we do if we hear them approaching?" asked Brochin, the camp tailor.

"Do nothing, just sit in the bunkers and pray quietly," came the answer.

Staying in the area became dangerous and soon they were evacuated. Once more they took apart their camp and moved, to reestablish it in a different location.

"Pack everything at once, we have to move," the instruction came one day.

"What happened?" everyone cried out. "Abandon the safety of the bunkers? Where will we go now?"

"To a different place. We are no longer safe here."

"Who said?"

"Our intelligence team."

"And who said that the Germans won't find us in the next place?"

"There is no choice," Shimaleh, the highest-ranking fighter replied. "We have to go deeper into the forest."

"What does 'intelligence' mean?"

"One of our Polish friends heard the village informants boasting that they know exactly where the camp is and the Germans paid good money for the information. We have to hurry, we will go during the evening. It is crucial that we leave nothing behind. The area has to be clean of any telltale signs."

So again Taiba, Yaakov Mendel, Shurka and Avraham packed

up their belongings, bundled their blankets and tools, covered the bunker, cleared away any evidence of their time there and when night fell, they followed the fighters.

In the new site, they had to prepare everything all over again: dig out the bunkers and the channels connecting them and prepare the camouflage from elm and oak branches.

"We never knew if we would stay in one place for a month, a day or a year," Shurka recounted, many years later. "But we became experts. Each time the move became easier. We were skilled and the baggage diminished as time went on."

"In a few days, Hanukkah will begin," Shurka told Irena. "Do you remember how we celebrated the holiday at Saba and Grandma's house?"

"I remember how Saba taught me to spin the dreidel that he made for me."

Shurka was quiet. Her heart ached with longing. She could barely hide her tears.

"Mama," Irena went on, "we will celebrate here. It will be fun. We will light candles in the forest and Grandma Taiba will make pancakes!" Taiba stroked her head.

"This year we won't make pancakes. We don't have eggs or oil for frying. But don't be sad. I promise you, next year we will celebrate the holiday in our house and I will make you one hundred pancakes."

"A hundred?!"

"We will make them together. You will be my pancake helper. You will help me peel and grate the potatoes."

Taiba and Shurka exchanged glances. How could they even think of next year when they were living in the forest, one day at a time?

"When Papa comes to visit us, I will tell him to bring us eggs and oil."

Shurka held back her tears. Those days, Avraham was wandering the forest searching for food and gear for his family, and only returned in the evening hours.

"Saba, could you build me a hanukkiah from branches?" Irena asked.

Yaakov Mendel's face crumpled. He did not want to worry the family with the fighters' concerns. They had explained to him that now they had to be especially alert. Holidays were particularly dangerous, since everybody knew that even in hard forest conditions, the Jews would gather together to celebrate. They would be busy with their rituals instead of security, which was an opportunity to kill as many of them as possible.

That evening Saba brought Irena a hanukkiah that he had made her from oak.

"It is a beautiful hanukkiah," said Irena, "make another one for my Alinka," and Saba laughed.

The first candle-lighting passed uneventfully.

They lit a little candle and immediately extinguished it so as to keep the complete darkness that security decreed. Inside the bunker, Shurka sang some holiday songs in a whisper, and Irena sang along with her.

Maoz tzur yeshuati... Mi yimalel gvurot yisrael...

"A great miracle happened there," her lips murmured, "Maybe we will also have a miracle."

The big raid happened on the night of the third candle.

The guards first heard the barking of dogs, still far away. It was clear that German forces were approaching. The instruction came immediately to secure the openings to the bunkers with their camouflage and stay silent. It was forbidden to so much as cough. They had to sit squeezed beside one another, no whispering, no eating, no drinking. Everything was dangerous.

"Iron discipline," said Rosin, one of the fighters. "Any one of us could cause the rest to be discovered."

Shurka covered Irena with a wool blanket and took her and Yitzhak down to their bunker. She instructed her daughter to sit beside her.

"Forbidden to speak," she told her. "Even in a whisper, do you understand?" Irena nodded her head to show that she understood. She understood so many things that children her age did not know.

Not half an hour later and they heard the barking of dogs and the shouts of soldiers. Everyone squeezed together in their bunker and prayed to God to protect their family. Suddenly they heard a weak cry. Yitzhak. The baby in Shurka's arms awoke and demanded food.

"Shh, my little chick. Stop my baby," she took him to her breast but Yitzhak refused to take comfort in his mother's protective arms.

"Quiet your baby!"

Shurka put her finger in his mouth hoping that he would be comforted. But his face was red and his cries did not stop. He was feverish.

"The baby is endangering all of us! You have to make him quiet!"

Shurka tightened her grip on his little body and pled with him not to cry... another moment, another hour and everything would be okay.

"Just don't cry, my baby. Please, baby, please. Relax, my son, don't cry," she whispered to him but the crying did not stop.

Someone lifted their camouflage cover and the head of one

of the fighters peered inside. "What's happening in here? Do you not understand that the Germans are close by?"

But Yitzhak cried. He did not understand.

"Quiet that baby," shouted someone from another bunker. "He will be the death of all of us."

Yitzhak responded with louder cries.

"Please, my boy, don't cry," Shurka put her hand over his mouth, pleading for him to stop and calm down. "Just for a moment. Please my child. Stop." But Yitzhak cried.

"Calm that baby."

"He will bring disaster upon all of us."

"Here is my son, Isaac, do not let harm befall him," she sent a prayer to the heavens and pulled her child in close, rocking him, begging for mercy. But the child went on crying. His face turned red.

"Quiet him, woman."

"He's going to alert the whole German army."

"Quiet over there!"

And Shurka put her hand over Yitzhak's mouth. "Shh, stop my child. Try to sleep. Dream of our home in the village, by the pear tree, think of the carnations..." and the cries softened until the bunker finally fell silent.

They sat in silence for half an hour.

The guards finally announced that it was possible to go out - the danger had passed, the German force had gone. The camp residents crept out of their bunkers one by one to give thanks for their good fortune. They kissed and embraced. This was their Hanukkah miracle.

Only one woman remained sitting. Shurka with her baby in her arms.

She gently rocked him and kissed his face.

"Get up my baby, the danger has passed."

Taiba and Yaakov Mendel were the first to understand what had happened. They rushed to her and tried to take him from her arms.

"Looks, he's sleeping. He doesn't want to wake up," Shurka tried to rouse him. She rubbed his little legs, moved his fingers, whistled to him. Maybe he had just fallen into a deep sleep and any moment now he would open his black eyes.

"Get up my baby."

But little Yitzhak lay lifeless in her arms. Taiba hugged her.

"Enough, give us the baby and come outside." But Shurka was stubborn.

"He will wake up, he is only sleeping! Why won't you wake up, baby?"

Hot tears rolled down her cheeks.

"My little chick... look, he's not even crying Mama."

"Give him to me my dear," Taiba begged.

"He wanted my comfort. But I couldn't protect him."

"You are courageous my dear. You saved all of our lives."

"I saw the ruler of the forest. He passed here and took Yitzhak's soul."

"He was ill," Taiba said, "he never had a chance in this place."

"He died for all of us... The child is a martyr," Yaakov Mendel tried to encourage her and Irena sat beside her and put her head on Shurka's lap.

"Forgive me, my beloved child," she pleaded. "Forgive me, and when you go up to heaven speak for all of us... tell whoever is there, hard-hearted, who takes no pity on his people, to wake up and give us a miracle."

"Mama, Mama, what happened to Yitzhak?" Irena asked, suddenly realizing something was very wrong. Taiba gestured to Yaakov Mendel to take the little girl away.

"Saba, what happened to my brother?" She repeated her question when he found a place outside for the two of them to sit.

"He went to sit among the clouds, with the angels."

"Mama said that the ruler of the forest took him?"

"No my little one, he—" For the first time in his life, Yaakov Mendel could not find the right words to answer his granddaughter.

"But what?" She could not understand with the logic of a child. "What did we do to the ruler of the forest that he is so evil? You said that he doesn't touch good children. Yitzhak was a good boy."

Yaakov Mendel's lips moved, whispering the ballad of the evil ruler of the forest who seeks the souls of young children."

Papa, Papa, I am caught!
Enmeshed by the forest ruler's plot!
The father groaned, his spirit stunned,
Put his hand on his hurting son,
But all was lost, as he got to the yard,
His boy was dead in his arms.

They buried Yitzhak that same night. They did not put a gravestone on his fresh grave, nor any marking that might, God forbid, give them away. They just dug him a small hole, befitting his tiny body, piled earth on top and covered it with fresh oak branches that the men had brought to cover the mound.

Shurka stood beside the small grave with heartbroken eyes, swaying from side to side as though she was about to fall upon the grave.

"God gave and God took away," said the cantor.

"Where were you?" Taiba screamed, "What kind of God are you?!"

Avraham stood beside Shurka, holding her so she would not collapse, his eyes sunken and his skin ashen with sorrow.

In a tired, defeated voice, Shurka said, "God you are wicked. You asked Abraham to sacrifice his son but you did not allow harm to come to the child, you brought a deer in his place. Why did you have to sacrifice my son, my only son, my beloved Yitzhak? He had a pure soul and never hurt anybody. Why didn't you bring me a deer? Why, God, why did you demand such a sacrifice from me? Why not take my soul too?"

The people of the camp remained silent. They felt helpless and wordless in the face of Shurka's pain.

Yitzhak died on the night of the third candle.

A great miracle did not happen there.

19.

January 1943.

The winter days were hard. The snow piled up and Irena's coat was already too snug on her. Her shoes pinched and hurt, so Shurka made an opening in them, allowing her toes to stick out and then wrapped them in a piece of a blanket she found to keep them warm...

"Look at the girl, she's growing like bread in the oven," Shurka smiled at Avraham who saw the pain in her eyes, which was at its worst at night. He knew that she was falling apart and saw she was wasting away in front of him. He determined to move his family to a safer and more comfortable hiding place, at least for the winter. He wanted to put some distance between his Sarah and the forest. Distance from the bunker where the tragedy had taken place might return a glimmer of the vitality that had disappeared from his wife.

Moreover, the trees that spread over them had already lost their leaves and stood naked, no longer protecting the people in hiding.

"Move again?" Shurka asked when Avraham told her to gather up their meager possessions.

"I arranged a hiding place for us. It's not good to stay in the forest in winter."

"Just not to a monastery." She had heard of monks opening

their doors to Jews but then trying to convert them.

"No, to a Pole."

"You said not to trust them."

"We have known each other for a long time."

"What about Mama Taiba and Papa... what will they do?"

"I'm sorry, the Pole is willing to take just us."

"I am not going anywhere without them," insisted Shurka. "One destiny for all of us."

"Go! We will be okay," Taiba assured her daughter. "Go with him. No Pole would agree to take in ten Jews and certainly not old ones like us."

Avraham asked her to trust him, that the Pole was a good friend. He did not tell her that he had given some of her jewelry and their silverware to the Polish peasant who had agreed to hide them in his granary.

His security chest had once again proven its value. These days it was hard to find anyone willing to risk himself. If caught, this offense was punishable by death - for the man and his entire family. Nonetheless there were those who were willing to take the chance in exchange for money, based on old family ties or idealists who saw it as an act of protest against the Nazi regime. No matter what their reasons for doing so, these Gentiles saved many lives and after the war many of them would be declared Righteous among the Nations.

Once again the little family set off in the dark of night, with the intention of getting to their meeting point before daybreak. Again they wrapped Irena in a big blanket, tucked a woolen hat on her head, covered her face, and rolled her up like a bundle. Avraham carried her in his arms.

Avraham knew the way well and he walked easily through

the forest, holding Irena and leading his wife. He knew exactly where to step.

When they neared Lejno, the Pole's village, dogs began to bark and a choir of cows answered them. But under cover of the darkness all around them, even those peeking out behind curtains were not able to spot them.

Avraham indicated to Shurka to stop and set Irena down.

"What now?"

"We wait. He will come."

Irena opened her eyes and looked at her parents but she did not complain or ask a thing. She already knew what it meant to be a refugee.

A few minutes later a figure came out from one of the houses at the edge of the village.

The figure approached them quickly and waved a hand to bid them to come closer.

"This is Yakob," Avraham pacified Shurka who walked beside him. "His father and I were friends."

"And you are certain that he—"

"Shhh," said Avraham. "Come, let's get moving."

The man gestured to them to follow him to the yard. There before them stood the big granary. He pointed to a tall wooden ladder and held out his arm to help Shurka climb up.

They did not ask questions or thank him. They just climbed quickly and sat between the high stacks of straw. At the far end of the granary were several folded blankets. They spread them out on the concrete floor and held hands in silence so that the neighbors would not notice, God forbid, that someone was there.

They spent the whole winter hiding in the granary.

They lived in complete silence, alert to all the everyday

noises in the house: the clinking of glasses, the clatter of cutlery, the sound of a chair being dragged across the floor, people's prayers. Outside they heard youths singing, the geese honking, and from afar they heard the farmers urging their cattle into their barns, the neighing of horses, the barking of dogs, the women calling to children to come home in the evening, and the grinding of wagon wheels on the gravel roads.

They knew village life well. Until not so long ago they had lived that life themselves.

It was only when the village went to sleep and every house had extinguished its lights that the peasant would join them. He would open his coat and pull out a loaf of bread, half a cabbage, a few carrots and half an apple, and promise that the next day he would bring a more substantial meal.

"You have to promise me you will stay quiet. Everyone here is watching everyone else closely - if they hear I am hiding Jews they will call in the Germans immediately."

They agreed that they could go out of their hiding place in the dark and stretch their limbs and walk about a little bit, but not to stray far from the granary entrance.

"You must understand, there is always some bad soul in the village," explained the farmer. "If they suspect you are here... it won't be just you in danger but my family too."

Avraham knew well that if, God forbid, the Germans should find them, Yakob and his whole family would be killed. That is what the Germans declared and that was what they did.

Avraham shook his hand and promised that they would stick to the rules.

"You are a good man," Shurka told him.

"I wish I could do more for you," sighed the farmer. "Your father Aharon was a friend of my father. He taught me how to ride a horse. It hurts me to think what they are doing to you."

"And your father once let me taste some beer, and I remember that my head was spinning and I didn't understand what had happened," Avraham laughed.

Yakob stroked Irena's head.

"How old are you?"

"Nearly five," the girl replied.

"Tomorrow I will bring you my daughter's old coat. She doesn't need it anymore and yours... I hope my wife won't notice. You probably understand, she is worried, afraid."

"Understandable."

"I wish I could do more for you."

"You are doing more than enough," said Shurka.

"Since I won't be coming here a lot, is there anything else that you need?"

"If you should happen to find a pair of shoes for the girl, her feet are growing so fast..." Shurka said. Yakob took her measurement with his fingers and promised to bring shoes too.

For nine weeks and five days, Avraham, Shurka and Irena hid in the big granary on Yakob's farm. They learned to live in silence, to move about their hiding place without so much as a creaking floorboard, to speak without words and to understand one another without making a sound.

"I forget what laughter sounds like," said Shurka, and Avraham assured her that they would laugh again.

Nor did they dare to cry. It was only when the night fell, like ghosts returning from the land of the dead, they would move their bodies a bit, whisper comforts to one another and eat the little food that the peasant had brought them. But not always. Sometimes two days would pass and the tiny portion of food did not come. Maybe Yakob saw Germans in the area. Maybe one of his neighbors had begun to ask questions. They could not go out to see what was going on. They could only wait in silence.

For nine weeks Shurka and Avraham had to keep Irena busy. They taught her to recognize the sound of the sheep's bells, the chirping of the birds and different smells. They taught her mathematics. Shurka would set down stalks of straw before her, adding and subtracting, all without words. They learned to communicate with glances.

The parades of ants fascinated Irena during the long hours when she had to remain silent, and they became her best friends. She watched their arrival every morning, followed them, placed seeds in their path and gave them names.

"This brown one is Mirosh, the limping one is Walde, and Stefania is the one who is always in a hurry. How are you doing this morning, my little ants? Where are you rushing to?" she asked them silently.

Under the cover of night, Irena would sit on Shurka's lap as she told her stories and taught her the works of the Yiddish poet Kadia Molodowsky which she remembered by heart from her own childhood. There was a poem about a deer and another about a blue umbrella, about the coat of Peretz Lutz, entertaining stories about Jerusalem and about golden feathers and "open the gate, open it wide, so the golden chain might pass inside..." and Irena recited after her.

And so they would pass the time until their eyes closed and they fell asleep. They learned to doze while remaining attentive to what was going on outside.

"Time works completely differently when you are in hiding," Shurka would later explain to her grandchildren who wanted to know how they had passed the time: hours and days and weeks in silence.

"There is no meaning except to be, to live, to survive another day, another hour. To awaken in the morning and see that you and your loved ones are still alive and well. That we are together. That was the purpose. What do you do? There is no such question - you just live, try to survive and go on living. And that was the most we could do."

On the ninth week, Yakob came up to visit them late at night. From his ashen face they could tell immediately that something had happened.

The farmer told them that the Germans were bringing reinforcements. The army and those cursed dogs of theirs were searching for Jews and the Poles who hid them, with assistance from the local population.

"I'm sorry," he said, not making eye contact.

"And you are worried?"

"Very much. There are people around here who would hand over their own mother for a bottle of vodka. Yesterday they burned down the houses of two farmers just because there was a rumor that they were hiding Jews. They said that's how they check if there were Jews inside, they would scurry out like rats."

"Did someone ask you about it?"

"The neighbors are beginning to be suspicious. I was informed that someone in the pub said that he thinks I am hiding Jews in my granary, that he saw shadows moving about at night, and that thanks to me he would get a reward."

"We understand, give us a few days and we will go," said Avraham.

"You must understand - I am worried for my own family. I'm

sorry, but you will have to leave tonight."

Shurka was quick to assure him, "Don't be sorry, you did more for us than we could have imagined."

"Go carefully, so nobody will know you are here. These days one can't know who might inform on you."

"Don't worry," promised Avraham, "we will leave before they get here. Tonight we will go, we will be okay. You are a righteous man."

"Can I do any last thing for you?"

"Yes," said Shurka, "end the war."

A smile rose on Yakob's lips.

"I wish I could."

"Maybe you can get us some warm clothes, old shoes, hats, a blanket," Avraham said. "Anything you could find would help us."

"I will bring everything, just please, do not tell a soul that I helped you. Otherwise... you know what they do to people who help Jews."

They knew all too well.

Not an hour had passed before a big package was thrown inside. They knew that the good Yakob had given them a parting gift.

Between the blankets and the heavy coats they found white socks with a red ribbon for Irena, inside of which he had tucked the jewelry that Avraham had given him.

"I will wear them when we get back to our house," she told her parents and gave the treasure to her father for safekeeping.

They left their hiding place exactly as they had entered it - secretly, under cover of darkness, and once more they walked towards the forest, to their hold home. Avraham held Irena in one arm and with the other, he held Sarah's hand.

When they got back to their forest camp, they saw the first signs of spring. The trees that had been bare when they left had begun to cover themselves with a fresh green coat.

"Good morning Jews," Avraham boomed in his big voice. Taiba and Yaakov Mendel ran toward them. Shurka froze for a moment, stunned by the sight of her parents, who had shrunken notably during the winter months.

"As though getting closer to the earth," the terrible thought crossed her mind.

20.

It was not only her parents that had shrunk.

The entire camp looked as though it had dwindled.

They saw that there were far fewer people, and a troubling silence prevailed. Devorah, Shurka's sister, hurried toward them. It was impossible not to notice that she too appeared thinner than ever; Shurka did not dare to ask if she had had her baby or what had happened.

"You know that..." Devorah tried to tell her, "in the middle of a snowstorm... he... he didn't have a chance... he was born and he didn't want to live here."

"My darling," Shurka stroked her face. "Maybe it's for the best. Who would want to bring a child into this world? Look at us..."

"They didn't even let me see him," Devorah sobbed. "When the contractions started they called a doctor... he slipped out quickly... didn't even cry... you understand, he didn't make a sound... he just didn't want to live in a world such as this..."

"This is no place for a baby," Shurka wiped away her sister's tears. "Now he is in heaven with Yitzhak, maybe together... maybe they will look after us."

"You are still young," Shurka continued. "Soon the war will be over and the children will come one after the next."

While Shurka and Avraham were trying to resume their familiar routine and mend the bunker after the snow, the fighters arrived with bad news.

The danger had grown. The Germans were benefiting from the cooperation of the peasants, the punishments for helping Jews had become more severe, and the Polish nationalist partisans posed a serious threat.

"Soon we will have to leave and build a new camp," the camp commanders informed them.

"I can't do it anymore," said Shurka. "I can't, I'm exhausted." She could hardly stand on her feet. The hard winter had weakened her.

Her family tried to encourage her, and treated her to hot soup and even an apple that Avraham had managed to obtain. On the third day her temperature rose and she writhed from strong stomach pains. Avraham and Yaakov Mendel summoned the camp doctor, Dr. Bucha.

"He was not really a doctor," Shurka explained years later, "but he had medical knowledge, sharp senses, and the ability to read his fellow man, and he managed to help a lot of people. All of us relied on him. They said he was a miracle-worker."

Dr. Bucha confirmed what they were afraid of... Shurka had contracted typhoid fever.

"You understand that without medicine..." Bucha's words hung in the air.

Avraham got up and left without hesitation.

A few gold coins were transferred to the pharmacist of the nearby village in the middle of the night and he returned with medicine and even a little fresh cheese and bread for the patient.

Ironically, it turned out that typhoid fever saved Shurka and her family.

It was 1943, in the month of Adar in the Jewish calendar - a month in which it is a mitzvah, a good deed to rejoice. Purim, a festive holiday, takes place in Adar.

They had no Torah with them, but they knew the stories from that month's holy book.

Since Shurka was weak, and since they did not want to leave her alone on the day of the festivities, the extended family gathered together in the bunker and told the Purim story of Esther: the tale of the rescue of the Jewish people from the great disaster hanging over them.

Aunt Alinka told Irena about Mordecai the Jew and Esther the beautiful, of Achashverosh the stupid kind of Persian, and about Haman the wicked.

"Maybe Hitler will face the same fate as the wicked Haman," Yaakov Mendel joked. "And all of us can see him hung from a tree here in the forest. I will tie him there myself."

"Amen and Amen," everyone answered, like after a prayer. They allowed themselves to smile.

Avraham sang the song of the clown who danced on the rope to Irena.

"The Germans!" They suddenly heard a cry from the family camp along with the sound of dogs barking.

"They're here, run!" someone shouted.

"To the bunkers!" directed someone else.

Most of the camp residents happened to be outside, busy with their own tasks, and they all began - despite the instructions to hide during a raid - to run away as fast as they could, deep into the forest.

Shurka and Irena, and with them Taiba and Yaakov Mendel were inside the bunker, keeping Shurka company. They heard the dogs, the sound of the machine guns and the shouting, and they barely breathed for fear of being heard.

Then the terrible smell of smoke penetrated the bunker and their eyes burned. It became impossible to take in air. From outside they could hear the terrible sounds of trees burning and cries of pain. Was everything going up in flames?

Who knew what was awaiting them beyond their bunker?

Even so, they stayed put, holding each other's hands, and praying that the fighting would not touch them, that their closed bunker would protect them.

It was one of the worst raids that Yehiel Greenspan's camp ever saw.

Once they realized they could not find the Jews, the Germans decided to burn the forest and force those in hiding to run from the flames straight into their bullets.

Many of the camp's residents were killed that night. It had become clear that the situation had gone from bad to worse. The forest that had been a lifesaver had now become a deathtrap.

The camp diminished. Of the one thousand people who had been scattered throughout the forest, only a few hundred remained.

"And so, from bad can come good. Thanks to the typhoid, we were saved," Shurka smiled in the retelling. "If I had escaped with the rest, if my parents had not stayed with me, who knows, all of us might have been murdered."

And indeed the entire family survived that raid.

When the Germans finally left, the Jews came out from hiding and began to look after the wounded and bury the dead. Afterward they abandoned the camp and set off to build a new one.

Again they were wandering with all of their worldly possessions on their backs - destitute refugees.

"The freedom holiday - was a calamitous holiday," Shurka would report years later, wiping away a tear. "We knew that the holidays were hard days, not celebrations, no longer full of joy but full of sorrow and grief."

Irena's hair had grown and Shurka would gather it into a long braid and tie it with a cloth ribbon she had found.

Sometimes Yorek Cholmsky, a friend of Avraham and Shurka, would come. He belonged to the fighters' camp. He was tall and handsome.

When he approached he would call out, "Hey, where is my favorite little girl?" and Irena would run to him. He would lift her up onto his shoulders and run around the camp.

"My uncle is coming!" Irena would say.

Shurka and Avraham would ask, "Why Uncle? He's not really your uncle." But Irena insisted. She waited eagerly for him to come.

"This is my uncle!" she insisted.

She didn't know that she was predicting the future, that one day her aunt Ruska would marry Yorek and the two would move to a kibbutz in the Galilee and go by the names Shoshana and Benny.

Passover was coming up. They had no matzah and no wine with which to celebrate their holiday of freedom. All they had was an old Haggadah, the Passover Seder book that Yaakov Mendel had managed to bring along. It was falling apart but it would do.

"We can celebrate without matzah," said Yaakov Mendel.

"I will ask the four questions," cheered Irena. "Saba, please!"

"Repeat after me," Saba Yaakov Mendel taught her, "*Ma nishtanah...*"

Irena learned to ask the four questions and added some of her own.

"Saba, if God brought the Jews out of Egypt, why doesn't he take us out of the forest?"

"He will get us out of here yet. Just stay faithful. Now repeat after me, '*Shebechol haleilot, ein anu matbilin...*'"

"*Avadim hayinu ('we were slaves')*," her father taught her to sing and she thought to herself, "Are we also free? When can we shout and ride bicycles? When can I jump in the river and skip rope like all the other girls in the world?"

"We have Uncle Moshe Yurvitz right?" said Irena, "So he can get all of us out of the forest."

"And we have an Uncle Aharon too," laughed Taiba.

"You wait, the redemption will come. Moshe will find us and get us out of here but in the meantime you need to prepare for the Passover Seder. We will celebrate this year without matzahs but with lots of hope."

And so it was that at the hour when the sun began to set, they sat down to dine in the silent bunker. They sang their holiday songs in barely a whisper.

The holidays were days of disaster. Now that it was not so cold anymore, the sun had melted the snow, and the Germans would return to their hunting, deep into the thick of the forest with the help of Polish informants, to find those in hiding.

In Shurka's bunker, the whole family crammed together in fear. Silently, they sang "we were slaves" in their hearts.

Grandma Taiba and her children, Yodel and Rachel with their children and many others joined them. There was a good chance that the Germans would not notice them, that they would pass right by their area without discovering that the belly of the earth was beating with fearful hearts.

Only Avraham, as usual, was somewhere else, on one of his raids to obtain food for his family and the camp.

The crowding was so severe, that there was not space for everyone. Shurka and Irena climbed onto an upper wooden shelf inside the bunker, closer to the entrance, and lay there in an embrace.

That wooden shelf saved their lives.

It seemed that this time the Germans had precise information. They heard a voice yelling, "*Juden, Juden*," and then the sound of hand grenades being thrown into the bigger bunkers. The grenades exploded one after another and the bunker became a deathtrap.

Shouting and cries for help mixed with the smell of scorched flesh, smoke and fire, as though hell itself had descended upon the camp. It looked as though nobody survived this invasion.

Even when the quiet returned and the moans of pain died away with the souls of people, Shurka did not dare to open her eyes. She stayed holding Irena who did not even cry.

"Mama, why is nobody speaking?"

Shurka did not answer. She knew that the quiet was an ominous sign.

"Why isn't Saba singing? Why isn't Grandma laughing?"

Someone peered inside.

"Is anyone there?"

They were the guards who had come to check who had been hurt.

"Are you all right?" the voice whispered. Shurka heard herself say that nothing was all right. In that same moment she thought, maybe all of us are together in heaven.

"Who else is with you there?" the voice asked.

"Irena, my daughter. I think that those below us, my parents... Uncle Yodel... Rachel... they're not moving... maybe something happened to them."

She heard voices, and a bright light suddenly swept the bunker.

"Come." Outstretched hands helped her up. Shurka carried Irena in her arms, and she passed between the bodies, trying not to step on anyone while also trying not to see, on the terrible pathway to the door.

"This way," said the voice. A strong hand was held out and pulled her out.

"Are you okay?" One of the fighters brought her some water.

"I'm not."

"Who else was there?"

"I think... I saw... nobody survived," Shurka said. "My mother, my uncle... they're not moving..." She couldn't continue; the words stuck in her throat.

"You are the wife of Avraham, right?" Shurka nodded her head yes.

"We must hurry to get word to him," said the fighter, "She doesn't look okay to me... shock."

"My father... Yaakov Mendel... He wasn't there with us, also my brother Shlomo. They tried to escape. Do you know what happened to them?" Shurka asked.

She looked at Yorek. Uncle Yorek. His head was bowed, his face ashen, and he avoided her gaze. She did not need any further clues to understand. Disaster followed disaster.

The family members and all of the relatives had been with them in the family bunker were all slaughtered in that terrible raid. Those who tried to escape, like the two Yaakov Mendels or Shlomo, who was sixteen, had been shot and killed on the spot. Only Shurka's sister Ruska (Roz), who had been with the fighters, had survived. She had been orphaned and separated from all her loved ones in one fell swoop.

Shurka remained sitting beside the bunker, waiting for Avraham to return from one of his raids in the villages. Her hand stroked the brush growing all around them but she did not cry.

Her eyes were dry, just as they had been on that night of the third candle of Hanukkah.

After they had buried the bodies of her loved ones, Sarah prayed from her heart, "My heart grieves, a sorrow fills my soul, and there is no silver lining, no opening, no comfort. Please, God above, your grace, from the depths of this forest I pray to you, I ask for your mercy, pure souls were extinguished, their good hearts and minds, you took them to your side because they were angels in life and in death. Here in the forest the days are dark and the nights are relentless. Show me a little bit of blue sky, show me a sliver of light because my heart is empty, like a dried-up riverbed."

"Mama," Irena approached her. "Don't be sad... you still have me. I will never ever leave you, we will get out of the woods together, stronger, more loving, and even Hitler won't frighten us, because you are our mother Sarah, the great, beloved mother."

Shurka smiled and held her child in her arms and kissed her tenderly and they sat together in a tight embrace and wept.

The other few survivors stood, crying silently. Their tears fell onto the soil of the treacherous forest and wet the rocks.

21.

Shurka lost the little optimism she had left.

The life that they had tried so hard to hang onto seemed pointless. She got more and more depressed. Outwardly it appeared she had learned to live with her great losses but inwardly she was still shaken to the core by the thought that it was only by chance that she and Irena, her only remaining child, had survived. It had been so close. And it had all happened so fast. One moment they were there, whispering the Passover song about the little goat and the next moment her parents, and so many other loved ones were gone forever.

She was haunted by those thoughts.

She could not sleep at night, afraid that the nightmares would return. She lay in bed for hours listening to the sounds of the forest. Every little murmur made her jump, every breath of wind made her clutch her sleeping daughter close to her breast.

Avraham saw her sad eyes, heard the sighs that she tried to conceal, and knew that she couldn't sleep. He tried to stay by her side as much as he could and go off on fewer missions.

The family camp was forced to relocate once more.

"Tomorrow at nine we get out of here."

"Where to this time?" they asked.

"Deeper into the forest. We have to get further away."

"That area is full of swamps!" cried one of the women, "we would be better off staying here."

"And wait for the Germans?" asked one of Greenspan's soldiers who had come to help the families prepare.

"Maybe it would be better, the swamps will be the death of us. They are worse than the Germans."

"Nothing is worse than them... Don't worry, we have excellent guides."

"They say that the war—"

"Leave the war to us, you look after the families."

Shurka did not ask. She did not argue. She sat on a big rock and looked at the place where her relatives were buried.

"Shurka," Avraham hurried towards her. "I already packed everything, tomorrow at dawn—"

"I'm not going anywhere."

"We have to, it's dangerous to stay here."

He tried, asked and begged but she refused. She did not want to leave the old camp and go on. She said that she had no energy left to start afresh, to build another bunker. And most of all, she did not want to leave the place where her loved ones were buried.

"What would your mother have said to do?"

"You go with the girl. Go, leave me here alone. I will stay and wait for the Germans. They will come and take what remains - me."

Avraham sat beside her and hugged her tightly. He saw defeat in her eyes. He was very worried about her. He felt that she had reached a breaking point and had lost the will to live.

Again Avraham knew what he had to do. He had to get her out of the forest and give her a few weeks of rest, of calm, of distance from this place.

And again some gold coins, a silver platter and his mother's diamond ring changed hands, relinquished to strangers.

They left the forest in the quiet of night. Avraham held Irena and Sarah, acquiescing at last, followed after them. It was only four hours to the planned hiding place at the home of the Dochlovitch family, another acquaintance from before the war.

Everything had been coordinated and organized. They had determined a schedule, planned the dates and gave a deposit to Yashek, the farmer who was to hide Shurka and Irena in the large granary behind his house.

"Here," Avraham pointed to the lit up farmhouse. "They are waiting for us."

Shurka looked blankly ahead as though she had not heard him. As though her life had already been taken from her.

"Look it will be good for us here. We will spend another winter in a safe place."

When they got to the house, Shurka stepped aside and Avraham advanced and knocked on the door.

"Who is there?" a voice inside asked.

"It's us," Avraham whispered. "We're here... please open up."

The Pole hurried to open the door.

His wife, Zoshia who, according to the plan, was supposed to be at her son's house in the village some distance away, stopped him. She was stunned.

"What is this?"

"This... this is our food for the coming year." He pointed at the diamond ring he had been given in exchange.

"It's also a bullet to the head."

"Nonsense, and besides, I promised—"

"You are not opening that door. I do not permit them to be let in to our home." She stood decisively between her husband and the door, her hands on her hips.

"What happened to you woman? It's Avraham and Shurka!

You know how much his father helped us during hard times. Move away from the door."

"You're crazy," said Zoshia. "I don't care. Send them away! The Germans are swarming all around and there is no shortage of informants."

"He paid me with a gold ring! We can buy a young cow and—"

"Return everything to them," she said and put her finger through the ring. "Just keep this."

"Don't interfere. This is men's business. Move, woman!"

"We have small children... don't you have mercy for them?"

"Just for a month, two weeks... let them in."

"If you hide them in our house, I will inform on you myself."

"And have me, your husband, killed?"

"I will say that we didn't know, they just broke in..."

"Just for one night."

In the end, Yashek brought Avraham and Shurka up to the granary.

But Zoshia would not back down.

"I see they have a daughter too."

"Small and quiet. You won't hear her."

"She will cry and shout and bring the whole German army here. You want all of us to die because of your Jews? If you don't get rid of them I will tell the Germans myself. At least my children will be saved."

At daybreak, Yashek went up to the hiding place. Avraham and Shurka were lying on a bed of straw hugging one another as though they were a single body.

"Good morning," Yashek said but did not look them in the eyes as he handed them fresh bread and strawberry jam. Afterwards he said that he was sorry, ashamed, but they would have to leave.

"My wife is not willing..."

"Nobody will hear us," pleaded Avraham. "We are used to living silently, just breathing." But Yashek explained that she was threatening to inform on them.

"I understand," Avraham cut him off, saving him the embarrassment. "We really are a danger to you."

"No," Yashek tried to soften the blow. "She is worried because there is a rumor that they are looking for Jews around here and it could be very dangerous for you."

"We will leave at night," Avraham promised. "I will need a few hours to arrange a new hiding place."

The farmer returned the bundle of gold coins. "Take this. Maybe somebody else will be more generous than I can be." Avraham did not ask what happened to the ring. He understood.

"We will go back to the forest," said Shurka.

"Not yet. I have another idea."

"Let's go back... you understand that in the end someone will turn us in..."

"You will see. Tomorrow everything will be all right. You have my word," Avraham said, calming his wife. He promised, but in his heart he doubted his own words. He knew that the winter was fast approaching and already there were strong winds blowing and the nights were cold. Shurka would not survive the coming harsh Polish winter.

That night, Avraham hurried to Bojki, a small village a few kilometers north of Ostrow Lubelski that he knew well from his business dealings. There the Lepopovitch family lived. The Lepopovitches had been business partners of his father many years earlier. The elder Cheslev was a principled man who did not hide his hatred of the Germans. He thought that they were destroying Poland, and that the race laws were an insult to every human being. He thought that the Jews were a blessing for Poland.

Avraham's instincts were not wrong.

Cheslev hugged Avraham and brought him a glass of warm wine and when he heard the story, he told him that his house was open to them.

The three of them moved to the new hiding place by night. This time, they did not have to walk over the rocks and stones with their torn shoes. Cheslev treated them well and gave Avraham a horse and wagon.

Cheslev Lepopovitch and his two young daughters took them in with open arms. As it was autumn and the workers were still using the granary, they fixed the attic, arranged the harvest piles, and brought up the animal feed to protect it from the rains. And so they had themselves a new hiding place in the attic of the house.

"But you must be careful of my wife," Cheslev said when he showed them the way.

"She doesn't know?"

"She is ill, very ill. It will be better if she doesn't notice you. In her dying days she has become religious. She may yet call a priest who would immediately run and tell the Germans.

"The priest..." said Shurka. "But we were always together, the Christians and the Jews."

"The world is not the same as it once was."

Although they were careful, and although they lived in silence as they were well accustomed to doing, the sick woman still heard noises, got out of her bed and saw Shurka and Avraham and immediately understood who they were.

She began to shout, "Cheslev, what are you doing?"

"They are our guests."

"Send them away, now! It's forbidden."

"Okay, tomorrow they will go."

"Not tomorrow, *now*! These are the Jews who crucified Christ."

"They are Poles... Avraham's family has been in Poland for three hundred years."

"Send them away! They will bring disaster upon us."

Her daughters took her back to bed, stroked her head and reassured her that the guests really would be sent away. But nobody in the house intended to do as she demanded.

For three months they stayed in their hiding place.

During the night they would come down, passing slowly by the door of the ailing woman who was suspicious of what was going on in the house, and join the other family members in the large kitchen, where they were given hot soup and slices of bread. They spent their days in the reinforced attic between old suitcases, children's clothes, and broken bits of furniture. But they felt safe and the winds did not touch them.

The moldy attic seemed like a magnificent palace to them. The rain did not enter, and at night they had warm, filling soup.

Shurka later told her grandchildren who sat around her, drinking in her words, "I learned that people can grow accustomed to anything. Maybe because of that we managed to survive the terrible, inhuman conditions that we faced. During the first days, it was hard for us to get used to living in the dark, to moving about under the low ceiling. We were afraid to budge, in case someone might suspect something. We didn't dare to cough or sneeze, just breathe. At the beginning we thought we wouldn't be able to make it but after a couple of days we got used to it, as though we had always lived that way. Humans are highly adaptive."

22.

At the end of March, as a benevolent sun warmed the air, they returned to the forest. They had to.

Yashek's wife was in worsening condition and many people came to say farewell to her. The house was filled with guests who came at all hours of the day and evening, and the family had to crowd in their cramped hiding place until the wee hours of the night. They worried that someone might - God forbid - hear noises and understand what was going on.

They could not endanger the generous family who, for neither reward nor compensation but out of the goodness of their hearts had opened their doors to them, offering protection.

Before Avraham's family left their hiding place, the girls brought them blankets, bread and a little cheese and water and promised to pray for their wellbeing. The good Cheslev hid them under a large pile of hay in his wagon and drove them a long way to bring them closer to the forest.

They even gave Irena a soft red horse toy.

"We will never forget you," Shurka said and Avraham knew that his beloved wife was improving. She was smiling once again, and he had even heard her sing a song to Irena about the bear running away from the bees.

At noon they stood before the entrance to the Parczew Forest.

Avraham knew where the family camp was now situated... it had moved again during their time away. In order to get to the new location they had to travel around the main route and trudge through the marshland. They were swarmed by a cloud of mosquitos and Avraham tore branches off of an elm tree and gave one to Shurka and one to Irena so they could swat them away.

"Papa, I have never seen such big mosquitos in my life," laughed Irena.

"Keep going and keep hitting them."

"Look, they aren't afraid of me. I want Bojki - it was good there."

Avraham took Irena in his arms, covered her with one of the blankets they had been given and ran with her.

"See? I can run faster than the mosquitos."

"My father is the strongest father in the world," said Irena. "And faster than the mosquitos!" Shurka laughed.

They arrived at the family camp later that night, exhausted, their bodies covered with red blotches. Some of the bites had become inflamed.

That same night Irena's temperature rose and Dr. Bucha was called to the bunker where they were staying. He rubbed a bad-smelling salve over her body.

"You see," laughed Shurka, "the smell is so bad, even the mosquitos are shocked and the swelling has gone down." Irena did not complain. She already knew that mosquitos were the least of her worries, that there were worse enemies in the world.

She smiled at the doctor and thanked him.

The family camp was quiet, almost hopeless. People walked around in torn clothes, their eyes deeply sunken in their sockets. After the ghettos had been cleared out, there had been nobody new to escape and join the forest people. Many had been killed in the frequent German raids on the forest, in addition to those who had succumbed to typhoid and other severe diseases. Although only weeks had passed since their departure, Shurka was horrified to see the extent to which the situation had deteriorated. For nearly two years these people had been going about in the same clothes which had been worn thin and hung like shapeless sacks over their emaciated bodies. Their shoes were tied with ropes to keep the soles from falling off. In the absence of proper sanitation, the stench of the camp was almost unbearable.

"Here," she said, taking some of the clothes that she had received. "These will be for everyone."

Irena saw her mother sharing their gifts with others and she understood. She took the blanket that the girls had given her and gave it to one of the women.

"You have a big heart," the woman told her.

"She has an old soul that has already seen everything in this life," said Shurka.

"But I won't give my Alinka to anybody," she hugged her doll.

Shurka and Avraham organized themselves in an empty bunker whose previous inhabitants had either run away or were no longer among the living. They did not ask and they did not want to know. Irena was now the only child in the camp and quickly became everybody's favorite.

The summer of 1943 did not improve their situation. The days grew warmer, the winds stopped altogether, and the heat and humidity were unbearable, particularly inside the bunkers, which were built to protect their inhabitants against cold and invasions, but provided very little fresh air. The swarms of mosquitos from the nearby marshes attacked them constantly, and the fruit on the raspberry bushes and mulberry trees withered. Furthermore, the Germans were scouring the forests in an effort to capture the Russian partisans and those Jews who remained in hiding.

Roz was the first to whisper to them that people were saying Hitler's days were numbered - that the Russians were beating him.

"Where did you hear that?" Avraham asked her.

"There are rumors that the German army is taking a beating in the east, but don't rejoice just yet. The Gestapo is still searching for Jews in the forest more intently than ever."

"Will they never give up?"

"Maybe the opposite," said Uncle Yorek who did not leave Roz's side for a moment. "Thanks to their losses against the Russians they need to show how successful they are against the remaining handful of Jews."

Yorek took Avraham aside and gave him new tasks. "Mr. Plenty" continued to serve as the chief supplier.

But things had changed in the forest. The growing numbers of Russian partisans were allies of the Jewish group, but there was one problem: the Russian soldiers loved to drink, and when they were drunk they would search for girls, so the Jewish women had to learn to hide.

"From the Germans, the Poles, the mosquitos, and now from them," Roz complained. "But, they are with us, and together we will be victorious. Just a little more patience."

Every so often someone who had escaped from the east would arrive in the forest and tell about the goings-on at the Russian front.

"Despite good news, we were wary of celebrating too soon," Shurka later reported. "Many rumors came to the camp, rumors of every kind. Of gas chambers, of extermination, deportation, murder... In the sad state we were in we did not dare to dream that someone would succeed in stopping the Nazis. We feared that by wishing for it we would prevent its happening. We went on with the daily routine of our lives, living in the moment, without thinking of what the future would bring. We survived but we did not know for what."

Yorek was now their contact person for everything that happened. The rumors of hard battles and of places liberated from occupation stirred up hope. Even Shurka would wait with Irena for Yorek's arrival.

"Our radio corps," they called him in jest.

Avraham would also bring them good tidings every now and then.

Once he even brought them a newspaper which bore the best news they had read in their lives:

To the Eastern Front the German army has been severely weakened following heavy losses and has begun a slow retreat to the Dnieper River while they carry out delay operations. The Soviets advanced in the industrial area of the Donbas, and by the end of September 1943, their forces reached almost the entire length along the Dnieper River. The Third Reich is beginning to crumble.

At the beginning of October the leaves on the trees turned deep reds and purples and then, as they had every autumn before, began to fall. Piles of leaves covered the ground and Irena would jump happily onto the leaf piles. The days grew shorter and the nights were cold. They felt the Polish winter approaching again.

Soon the temperatures would drop and snow would cover the forest. Avraham and Shurka knew that the chance of their survival in their current physical state was small.

"I won't survive another winter," she thought and looked sadly at Irena who was pleased by every golden leaf she found. In the winter it was harder to find food and medicine. The harsh weather was a cruel enemy - no less so than the Germans.

The camp continued to thin out.

There were those who escaped as winter came on and, like them, found shelter in farmhouses. There were those who fled east toward the Russian forces or partisans. And there were those who succumbed to the cold, to illness, to hunger and died. There were new graves every day.

They heard that the war was about to end, that the Germans were retreating. The Russians were advancing. Hitler was losing. Freedom was close, but when?

The end was not yet in sight for the forests' inhabitants. Avraham and Shurka decided that they must arrange for the winter and again find shelter in the home of some Polish farmer. They still had a little jewelry and silverware that Avraham had so wisely managed to hide.

Toward the end of November, Avraham set off once again to find them a hiding place and arrived at the home of the Vilansky family at the edge of the village of Nowy Orzechow. Slava and Yezhiga's children had grown up and left them alone on their little farm. Slava's eyes sparkled when he heard what Abraham was willing to pay. His wife wanted to bargain.

"Also the girl? Impossible, no children!" She paused and waited for the offer to increase. "The girl knows what it means to hide," Avraham told them. "I will add the silver candlesticks.

They are antiques and certainly worth a lot."

"It's not enough," the Polish woman said. "You know that we are risking ourselves, that the Germans will kill the both of us if we are caught. I don't want the child in our house."

"You have nothing to worry about. My wife and daughter are familiar with living in hiding. You won't hear them - this is not the first time. And just for the lady Yezhiga, a ruby ring that will fit your fingers."

The Polish woman hesitated. Why give up now? Maybe she would be able to squeeze something else out of him.

"I don't know. Jews have a certain smell and if - God forbid - the dogs should pick it up..."

"Enough, woman!" Slava lost his patience. "I decide. It's fine, throw in a few more gold coins and the girl will come with you."

"I am willing to throw in a few more if you can take care of food for us as well," said Avraham. He saw the glint in their eyes and knew that they would not refuse.

Yezhiga held her husband's hand and pulled him after her, as though trying to prevent him from giving in too easily.

"Wait, maybe there are earrings too."

"Enough, he has nothing!" her husband spat in disgust.

"Send them away!" she shouted suddenly.

"Listen," Avraham approached them, "there are rumors that the Germans have suffered serious losses and are being defeated at the Eastern Front. When the time comes, it will be to your credit that you hid Jews in your home."

"And until the Germans leave, the Poles are searching for Jews and handing them over for vodka."

"The Poles aren't stupid. They know that the end is near and that everyone who cooperated with the Germans will be punished."

Slava and Yezhiga knew that what he said made sense. With

news of the events on the front, collaborators had begun to worry about their own fate.

They sealed the deal with a handshake, including sleeping arrangements, the food they would be brought, and the gear that they would need to stay the winter. Slava even agreed, in exchange for Shurka's wedding ring, to meet them halfway and take them to the farm in his wagon. Shurka would not have been able to handle the bumpy road. They set the date, the first of December, and marked the meeting point on a map. Now Avraham could return to the family bunker to tell Shurka that they would be safe in a refuge away from the dangers of winter in the forest.

Their new hiding place was perfect.

The village of Nowy Orzechow was far away from the main road and from other settlements. No one unfamiliar with it would ever encounter it. Around the village there were boggy swamps so the Germans did not frequent the area.

They arrived at the agreed-upon meeting place early in the morning.

Slava helped them up into the wagon and covered them with piles of hay. They stopped beside the house to leave the wagon, as though by chance, beneath the big granary that stood on wooden stilts that disappeared into the house. Everything was as they had agreed. They waited a few minutes, got out of the wagon, then climbed up the wooden ladder into the spacious barn. They found blankets and a jug of water hidden in a corner behind piles of hay at the back of the structure.

The routine in the new hiding place was familiar. They slept in an embrace to keep up their body heat, and were silent through the daytime hours. They tried to learn to recognize the people of the village from their voices and the local children whom they heard on more than one occasion playing directly beneath the barn.

While they were hiding in Nowy Orzechow, Shurka began to teach Irena to read and write. She was already six years old and Shurka, who continued to hope that the war would end soon, had begun to look ahead to the future. Avraham saw this as an excellent sign that his wife wanted their daughter to be able to join the class of children her own age. They practiced writing on the wooden floor of the granary, arranging letters from the grains of wheat.

Irena also made a new friend - a chicken with brown and yellow feathers. Nobody knew how she had gotten into the granary, but one morning Shurka woke up in alarm. Someone was pecking at her hand. She jumped up and found herself looking into the eyes of a spotted chicken who was as surprised as she was at the unexpected company. They looked at one another, taking in the new situation. Then Irena woke up.

She got closer to the surprising guest and without hesitating, hugged her. The chicken seemed to be fine with it.

"She came to me," Irena explained to her parents.

"Maybe she thinks you are her mother," Shurka laughed. And so a love was born between them and the creature who had found their hiding place. The chicken would wake them up with the dawn and disappear during the night - which is why she was given the name "Chort" (spirit, demon). Avraham would laugh and say that maybe she was their guardian angel. Now Irena had something to watch all morning. She would stroke her feathers, talk to her and tell her about everything that had happened to them.

One day Chort disappeared. Irena and Shurka searched the barn for her, called to her quietly, asking her to come back, preparing grains of wheat and water for her. After some time, Shurka gestured for Irena to follow after her, her finger over her mouth indicating not to speak. There, under a wooden table was Chort, sitting on two eggs.

"A good sign - spring is coming," said Avraham. "Maybe soon we can return to the forest."

23.

Avraham and Shurka knew that there were other Jewish families hiding in Nowy Orzechow.

It was a secret that they were forbidden to mention, even within earshot of Slava and his wife. Later it became clear to them that one of Shurka's friends, Bila Devorah, had been hiding there too, not far from them, since the beginning of the German occupation.

"You must understand, the game then was survival," Shurka's eyes saddened when she later told her story. "Each hiding place was different, everyone tried to find his own lifeline. There were those who hid in moldy cellars, and there were people crammed into narrow cells, and only at night could they go out for an hour to stretch their legs or do their business. There were those who hid children in big baking ovens or cupboards, in sewers or in bags of vegetables. Any possible place that a child could be hidden was considered and was, of course, well remunerated. Many children were hidden in monasteries, even though we knew that the priests would try to convert them to Christianity. A large number of those children returned to their families after the war, some no longer remembering their Jewish roots."

The barn was relatively comfortable. During the wee hours

of the night, Avraham would quickly descend the ladder and meet with other Jews.

They would send each other news or plan where to go to find food. That was how they maintained contact with other people from the forest and how Avraham learned that the Russians had dropped weapons to the Russian partisan units. From them he heard about the frequent attacks against the German convoys and about the damage done to their supply channels. Despite the frightening rumors of the Russian soldiers who would get drunk at night and harass the women and abuse the elderly, there was an optimistic feeling. Gestapo soldiers stopped harassing the local populations and their presence was barely felt, but other dangers did not diminish.

"We must beware of the Poles," Avraham emphasized to his friends. "Compliancy is the father of disaster in situations like this."

In spite of the feeling that the war was entering its final stages, and despite the trickle of good news, the situation in the village was bad. The long years of war had depleted the farms. Cattle had been slaughtered by the German army or had died of hunger. Fruit was stolen off the trees before it ripened, and the long winter months had left the peasants' cellars empty of potatoes. Even fishing from the lake barely yielded a thing.

It was as if the whole world had begun to perish.

Hunger was inseparable from the fabric of life.

From time to time Slava would bring them half a loaf of bread and a little tea.

"We also have nothing," he replied to Avraham when he descended to see if it was possible to get some fruit or vegetables.

"Look, we don't even have a piece of carrot to make soup for ourselves." He added in a sly tone, "It's no secret that Jews are experts at stealing food. Maybe you should go out and bring something for us too..."

So Avraham was forced to leave the hiding place to supply food to his small family and to others as well. His two partners in this task were brothers from the village, Moshe Oulitz and Nahum Dolik, who spent part of their time in the forest.

They knew each other well, worked effectively together, relied on one another and decided to look after Jews who were hiding in the village.

Since the farmers in the swamp region really had nothing, they began to travel by night on the roads to raid farther, more established villages. They picked fruit, milked goats, and carried off sacks of potatoes and the occasional sausage or jam from cupboards they found unlocked.

"You are putting yourselves in danger," Slava would warn them. "The Germans may be less active but remember that they are not your only threats. There are people from the Krayova Army in the region and they are known as Jew-haters; they won't hesitate to shoot you."

"We know them," Avraham would answer him. "Luckily for us, they are more afraid of us than we are of them."

"Just so long as they don't find out that I helped you," Slava voiced his concern. "They also shoot people who give Jews shelter."

"Don't worry," Avraham assured him. "Your secret is safe. We will never betray you."

At the end of April, Irena got sick. Her temperature rose quickly and she could barely breathe. Avraham went down to the house and returned with a bowl of cold water and some towels. All night they tried to bring her temperature down as she got weaker and weaker.

"Take this," said Shurka and placed a large bundle in Avraham's hands. "Ask them to call a doctor."

"No, I can't."

"Life is worth more."

Avraham knew exactly what Shurka had given him. Since they had left their home two and a half years earlier she had been carrying it with her. It was her sewing machine. All those long months she had refused to give it up, arguing that after everything was over, when life returned to normal, they would be able to rely on her hands and talent to get by.

"Are you sure?" Avraham hesitated but Shurka knew that this was their last hope.

"Yezhiga knows that a sewing machine is worth more than silverware. It's a profession. Ask that in exchange Irena can stay in their room and we will get the medicine."

And that was how it went. The doctor was summoned quickly to treat Yezhiga's "niece," Slava acquired the medicines, and on the second day Irena woke up and asked for food. They knew that her life had been saved.

Shurka never regretted that transaction.

"It was as though the finger of God had prevented me from selling the machine earlier in order to keep it for the hour of greatest need. I had to protect my child."

But she was not able to save Avraham.

One night Shurka woke up and by the lamplight in the room, she saw that Avraham was wearing his heavy wool coat. In a sleepy voice, she asked, "Why are you going out?"

"Shhh.... go back to sleep," he smiled in the darkness.

"Wait," she held out her hand to him and got up. "Don't go out tonight. Just yesterday you brought three green apples and half a loaf of bread. We have enough."

"But think of the others."

"I heard shots... maybe don't go?"

"You have nothing to worry about," he hugged her. "I am the king of being cautious. You won't finish your first dream before I'm back."

Shurka watched her husband. In these past few hard years, he seemed to have shrunk a little. His beautiful eyes were sunken and his face was ashen but determined. His mouth was pursed as if to say he was not afraid of a thing. Shurka was worried but she stroked his cheek and remained quiet.

"You trust me, right?" Avraham placed his hand on Shurka's hair. "Sarah, my queen, I have gone out hundreds of times and every time I come back to you healthy and whole."

Shurka shook her head as though asking him not to tempt his good luck.

"Maybe," he added, "maybe this time I will find a hairbrush for your beautiful curls."

"Please stay," she whispered. "I don't need a brush, I just need us to stay together."

"We will stay together always," he promised. "Just tonight I must go out. Tomorrow we will celebrate Shavuot together. I will try to find some fresh fruits so we can perform the offering of the first fruits."

"Please," Shurka pleaded. "You know that the holidays are disastrous. And they say that the end of the war is usually hardest."

"The Germans are being defeated in the east, the Russian partisans are multiplying from one day to the next. The end is near, and maybe this will be our last Shavuot that we have to celebrate in hiding."

"Amen," Shurka was quick to say. "But please, don't go out tonight."

She herself did not understand what had gotten into her that she kept pleading, but her heart was predicting some calamity...

"Enough!" Avraham said impatiently. "I have to hurry. The night is dark and the moon is still small. I'll go and I will be back before you even wake up."

In the morning, when she awoke, she touched the pillow on the mattress beside her. Avraham was not there.

That afternoon, Slava came up to see them.

As soon as she saw him, she understood.

She did not say a word, did not cry out, just looked at him with lips tightly pressed together. The worst had happened.

The villagers reported that the night before, soldiers of the Polish Krayova Army had killed three Jews who had attacked them, or so they claimed.

"It's not yet certain that it was Avraham," he qualified.

But Shurka knew. A loving heart does not err.

She found no solace in the story of Avraham's friends' vengeance on the Poles, catching the murderers and later on, bringing them to trial. Avraham had known that the end of the war was drawing near. He had predicted that liberation was close at hand.

"Why, God, why—you are the one who told him 'go to the land that I will show you.' You brought Abraham to the land that you promised him and you made him a great nation. Why, God, didn't you do the same for my Avraham?"

The next day, when they knew for certain who had been killed. Slava and Yezhiga climbed up the ladder and sat across from Shurka and Irena. Yezhiga wrapped a big wool scarf around Shurka's shoulders and placed new cloth shoes beside her.

"Thank you," Shurka said and Yezhiga burst into tears, moved by Shurka's silent suffering.

"I'm sorry... maybe we did not treat you as well as we should have. We only thought of ourselves."

Shurka gripped the outstretched hand.

"We understand. The Germans shoot anyone who hides Jews."

"Him and his children. And the informants can't wait for the chance to turn someone in. Please don't be angry with me." She hugged and kissed her, but she did not return the ring.

Slava handed her a package that contained a loaf of fresh bread, cheese, and some jam.

Shurka did not touch the food.

"Eat," Slava told her. "You need strength, a lot of strength."

"I don't need anything anymore."

"Don't forget, you have Irena, and she has you."

Shurka pursed her lips. She did not want the Poles to see her crying.

"How can we help you?" Slava asked.

"I want to return to the forest," Shurka whispered.

"Why?"

"I have friends there, and relatives. Their fate, mine, I can't stay here alone."

Yezhiga tried to convince her that they would best off staying but Shurka was determined. The loneliness, the long hours without anyone to help, to share, were more than she felt she could bear. Though of course she couldn't share her concern, she was also worried that Slava and his wife would eventually give in and betray her.

Life in the forest had taught her not to depend on anybody.

Slava volunteered to return Shurka and Irena to the camp.

It was already spring. The sun had melted the snow, the trees were budding, and Shurka breathed the fresh air deep into her lungs.

"We will be all right," she whispered to Irena.

"All of us. Even my doll Alinka."

When they parted, Yezhiga tucked some sandwiches into Shurka's pocket. She once again rolled Irena into a blanket, bundled her hands in some wool, and put a big scarf on her head. Shurka thought she saw tears in Yezhiga's eyes.

On the way to the forest, Shurka sat beside the farmer, her head covered, and dressed as a Polish peasant. She held her head high, her lips clenched, and she scanned the areas they passed with concern. She was now the head of her family, mother and father to Irena. Both of them had lost everyone dear to them in the war.

And there was someone else in the wagon.

Only when the village had disappeared was the secret revealed.

Chort was traveling with them.

She was held tightly and well hidden under the wool coat that Slava and his wife had given to Irena.

"What do I hear?"

"It sounds to me like a chicken," smiled Slava who was in on the secret.

"Will you allow it?" asked the girl with eyes wide with disbelief and hugged the chicken.

"She's your friend right? So yes."

"This chicken brought happiness that we thought had disappeared forever," Shurka later recounted.

They joined the moving shadows that remained in the camp. Walking dead.

They did not know that the Eastern Front had been resolved, that the Germans had retreated to the German border, leaving ruined cities behind, that the battle was over.

Twenty-two days later, at the end of July, they could vacate their bunkers at last, leave the forests and return to look for the Poland they had lost.

24.

July 1944.

In the family camp, they began to feel the change. At first they heard but did not dare to believe it... hope was something that belonged to free people.

Intellectually they knew what was happening, but it was the kind of feeling that the body recognizes first... relief.

They spent long hours outside the bunkers. They spoke at full volume, unafraid, and when Irena sang to her doll Alinka, nobody quieted her.

It had already been several weeks since anybody had looked for them, or since anyone had heard the sound of fierce dogs barking.

Now they could walk through the forest undisturbed, and the Polish peasants that they met on their way actually smiled. Some even offered them fresh food or milk.

Another week passed and with the approval of the fighters, they slept outside the bunkers, in the fresh air, their limbs stretched wide over a carpet of leaves.

In the small camp they could hear the planes overhead and feel the earth shaking under Russian tanks that were not far off. They knew liberation was close but they were still afraid, particularly apprehensive about the future life they would have outside of the forest. They were worried that the Germans might return, about the Russians who had conquered Poland, also about the Poles themselves.

"Remember, whatever happens, it's important to stay together," the fighters instructed them. "When the liberation armies come, don't scatter, just listen to their instructions."

Shurka did not know how, in her terrible loneliness, she would continue her life. Without her parents, her brothers, her husband.

"My Avraham," she whispered to him at night. "If you were here with me, you would know where I have to go. Please give me a clue, a hint."

One day, Shurka took Irena to the little river which flowed near the camp and they bathed in the cold water. Then she washed their clothes which had not seen soap for months. When the time came, they wanted to be presentable.

Sunday, July 23, 1944, was the day when the people of the Parczew Forest were liberated.

The command to move came from the fighters' camp.

"Where to?" someone shouted.

"I am afraid, they will turn us in."

"Don't ask too many questions," said Shurka, who remembered what Avraham had taught her. "Just keep moving forward. Only forward."

The dozens of survivors began to march, leaving behind the graves of their loved ones who had been killed or had died from starvation or illness. They also left behind their memories... but those would continue to haunt them for the rest of their lives. Under the fighters' commands, they took everything they could handle: torn blankets, pathetic bundles that now constituted all of their earthly belongings.

Irena held Chort in her arms. She refused to part with her.

The chicken looked festive, her small head bobbing quickly

back and forth as though trying to understand what was happening.

"Where are you taking her?"

"She too is liberated today," said Irena. Shurka explained to her that it would be better for the chicken to remain in one of the villages where they could take good care of her.

They turned toward the first village by the forest, only to find an enormous Russian tank blocking the way. They covered their heads with their hands and waited, tensely. They did not dare to look.

After all, a tank meant death, a soldier meant gunshots, fire, grenades.

Yet a friendly head appeared out of the tank, and then two Russian soldiers got out and smiled at them. One of them even offered a cigarette to Yorek who was walking beside Shurka.

Was this a good sign or a bad sign?

Better not to ask, not to know.

One of the officers gestured for them to follow him. The survivors marched beside one another to the center of the village, where Russian trucks were parked.

"Here," the officer indicated to them, "get into the trucks."

Was this some new trap?

Clearly... now they were taking them to some other prison.

The soldiers approached, but did not push. Some gave them a little water, fresh bread, even sausage and apples. A Russian soldier offered Irena a square of chocolate and Shurka, who finally felt she could trust these men, whispered to her to take it, not to be afraid.

Irena looked at the square of chocolate and licked it slowly. She hoped to make the taste last for many hours, days, months, years.

"Thank you, here take her," said Irena, handing Chort to him. "Will you take good care of her?"

The soldier smiled.

"Don't eat her... she brings luck!" Shurka told him.

The soldier, who did not speak their language, looked embarrassed. He looked from the girl to Chort, then suddenly appeared to know what to do. He turned around and gave the chicken to a youth who looked like a local villager. He smiled at Irena.

"She brings luck," Irena told him in Polish.

Without any unnecessary questions, the youth took her in his arms and hurried away.

"She's called Chort," Shurka called after him before he disappeared.

"I'm getting in," someone whispered, and they began to climb onto the trucks, trusting the soldiers.

"We sat in those trucks and we felt the wind hit our cheeks," a smile lit up Shurka's face when she later described that day. "It was the first time that we had left the forest during the daytime, without having to be afraid. It was the first time in years that we could hold our heads up, feel the fresh air and not have to hide. The people around me were still stunned. Not one of us dared to laugh or cry. Nor did we ask any questions. We had learned from experience and waited to see what they would do with us. We worried. The Russians were nice to us and shared candy and fresh bread. They tried to calm us, but we wanted to be sure that this was not some sort of new trap. Every now and then I would touch Irena's face, kiss her fingers, and check that this was really real."

"This is the way to Lublin," one of the survivors next to Shurka whispered to her. "I wonder why they are taking us there."

Shurka had never been to Lublin before but she had heard about it many times from her father and from Avraham. She knew that Lublin was home to a big Jewish community. Interesting, she thought, how many Jews would be there now.

The trucks stopped next to the municipality building, where they were told to get off.

At the entrance there were decorated tables waiting for them and Polish women served them hot soup and fresh bread with smiling faces. Irena let go of Shurka's hand and ran ahead to one of the tables. A woman in a white apron told her not to get any closer.

Irena put out her hand and turned to look at Shurka, "Smell that Mama... soup in bowls! With spoons!"

They hugged their bowls of soup and sat in a corner. A soldier passed between them and handed out clean blankets, towels, and a wedge of white soap. Liberation was real. Not a dream or a faint hope. They spent the night in a school that had been converted to house the refugees.

In the morning everybody went to the Jewish community center.

"The war has not yet ended," the community leaders explained. "They are still fighting in the west. Our brothers in the concentration camps are still being sent to their deaths. You are lucky to have been liberated."

Lublin became a center for Jews that had gone into hiding in the forests; Jewish partisans and refugees who had hidden in the cities or villages, those liberated from the concentration camps. Among the latter were the many from the countries of

Western Europe who saw Lublin as just a transition stop until they could return to their homes. To them were added Jews who had served in the Red Army or the Polish army. Together as one, they turned to the local council to register in case anybody should inquire about them, and to pore over the existing lists in the hopes of finding names that they knew. The first priorities of the council were: welfare, food, clothing, housing, as well as medical and legal assistance.

25.

Shurka and Irena stayed in Lublin for two days. They walked around the city, spoke with other survivors, and learned about the locations of others. They tried to find out if anyone had seen Yorek or Ruska, whom they had lost track of when the Russians moved them to Lublin.

On the third day they joined a handful of Jews who returned by train to Parczew -

"Why to Parczew?" Irena asked Shurka.

"I am almost certain that Ruska is there."

"Why?"

"I saw her name on the lists."

"What will we do there? Let's go look for our house in the village Mama."

"We can't. We have to stay together. They told me that many survivors are going to Parczew and building a new community. It's not good to be alone."

But Satan had not released his grip on the Jews just yet.

After the war, Parczew was among the few *shtetls* (towns and villages of Jewish populations) where an attempt was made to reestablish the Jewish community; at the beginning of 1946, there were about 200 Jews in the town.

They believed that this was to be the golden age of the Jewish community.

But in February of that same year, the local anti-Communist

partisans took over the town and carried out a pogrom; three Jews were killed, and most of the houses destroyed. After those events, most of the Jews left the town altogether.

At the train station next to the town, a cart waited to take them to the Jewish quarter, about 2-3 kilometers from the station. They arrived at their destination in the evening hours.

"Here we can find friends and relatives and not be alone," Shurka explained to Irena. She knew where to look.

She searched for her relatives' house, which she remembered from a photo Taiba had once shown her as a two-story stone house with five steps in front and a stone statue of a lion on the right.

"You see here?" She could hear Taiba's voice as she pointed to the house in the photo. "This is where my sister and her husband live. One day all of us will go visit them in Parczew."

It was a harsh sight that greeted them when they stepped down from the cart.

Most of the Jewish quarter's wooden houses had been burned. The trees in the yards stood bare and sooty from the explosions.

"Where, Mama?" asked Irena and Shurka explained to her that she knew Ruska had left the forests before them and was living in the family house.

"I saw the lists in Lublin. Ruska and Uncle Yorek are here."

"Uncle Yorek?" Irena's face lit up.

Shurka laughed, "He is like part of the family now."

Irena looked at her mother and felt happy. She had not heard that laugh for years.

"And we have a house here?" she marveled.

"We don't. It's my uncle's house. I know what it looks like... you can't mistake it. I am sure that my sister Ruska is here."

"How will we find the house?"

"My mama always said that it was not far from the big syna-gogue in Parczew. Look for a sculpture of a lion."

"And if we don't find it?"

"You have good eyes, you must help me look for a big stone house with an iron gate and a big apple tree beside it and a lion near the entrance. You can't miss it."

They walked around for hours but found no stone house.

"Mama you are confused," Irena laughed. "There are only wooden houses here."

"Wait and see," Shurka stroked her head. "I clearly remember from the photograph: stairs and two lions, one on each side... that is how we will find the house."

As they continued on their way they had to step over many fallen beams, broken furniture, piles of rocks that once made up the walls of houses.

They walked around streets with no houses and the skeletons of old huts until Irena shouted, "Mama, look, there, a stone house and metal gate... but there are no lions!"

It was the house she remembered. This is where she had wanted to get to.

"You see!" Shurka laughed. "I remember what Mama Taiba told me, that it was the most beautiful house in all of Parczew. I guess the lions were damaged in the fighting."

They climbed up the five steps and stopped before a cracked wooden door.

"Look Irena," Shurka held her hand excitedly, "we will enter through the front door. And if we want, we can shout! We can shout loud, we don't have to be afraid anymore - nobody will turn us in or call the Germans. Come, let's shout together. Let's see how nice it is."

And Shurka lifted up her head and shouted, "Ruska! Ruska!

We're here!" The two of them called out and knocked on the door. "Ruska, where are you? Ruska, my dear sister, open up, it's Shurka and Irena!"

They stopped for a moment to listen. Shurka heard steps hurrying toward them and her heart began to pound.

"Irena? My little one, is it you?" Yorek's voice could be heard from inside.

"That's Uncle Yorek!" cried Irena excitedly. "He didn't forget me!"

Moments later Irena was riding on Uncle Yorek's back just like in the old days, stroking his broad neck and Shurka was embracing her sister.

The beautiful and spacious home that Taiba had described was in ruins. The walls were bare. Everything had been torn down and destroyed. Nothing was left.

"This is how it is everywhere," said Yorek when he saw the look on Shurka's face. "The Poles... from the moment they kicked the Jews out they took everything they could steal from the houses. And when they finished they burned everything. Luckily this house was saved. In a few days we can start to get organized and rebuild."

"We knew you would come," Ruska said and handed them a cup of steaming tea. The familiar smell reminded Shurka of her mother. "We heard that they moved everyone who remained in the forest to Lublin. We left you a message. We didn't know when you would get here. We thought you might stay there for a bit."

"I looked through all the lists looking for relatives but I only found Yorek."

"You couldn't have found me, I'm now known as Shoshana Rozenski."

"What?"

"Yes," Ruska smiled. "We were married two weeks ago in the forest. One of the partisans who is also an ordained Rabbi did the ceremony. Instead of a *chuppah*, we stretched an army blanket from four rifles."

"And I didn't even know," whispered Shurka.

"That's right, we didn't tell anybody... Sorry."

"So many dead and you already had a wedding?"

"We have to find reasons to celebrate, Shurka."

"But we haven't even had the chance to grieve..."

"Enough grieving, the world is different now Shurka. Life is going back to normal, we must move on, not look back."

"That's what everyone wants," Yorek hugged his young wife. "Everyone who survived that hell, all the survivors, now they want to start families."

Shurka was quiet a moment.

"I'm sorry, you're right." She laid her hand softly on her sister's arm. "People lost so much and now they want to fill that void."

"Exactly! We must triumph over the horrific memories."

Thoughts of pregnancy, friends and family left behind were too hard.

"Not many returned," Ruska broke the silence. "Hardly two hundred people. Those monsters took everyone to Treblinka..."

Shurka pointed at Irena, hinting to her sister not to continue.

Ruska placed a blue bead in Irena's hand.

"In the yard you will find many beads like this one, and tomorrow we can make a necklace. Go see how many you can find," and she went, leaving the adults free to continue their conversation.

"We set up beds for you," said Uncle Yorek. "It's no palace

but compared to the forest everything feels like a palace. And most importantly, we have a shower! The water pressure isn't strong but compared—"

"Compared to what we had in the forest, it'll be a magnificent waterfall!" laughed Shurka.

Suddenly a feeling washed over them that everything would be alright.

That night, after more than two years, Irena and Shurka slept in separate beds. It was strange for Irena to fall asleep out of the arms of her mother, away from her sweet scent. When she woke up it was still dark in the room. She saw her mother standing by the window. She did not ask but understood that she was crying.

"Mama?" she whispered.

"Keep sleeping, Irena." Shurka answered in a cracked voice.

"Are you crying, Mama?" Irena asked her in the darkness.

Shurka could not answer. The tears were stuck in her throat.

"Please Mama, you don't have to be sad. You'll see, everything will be fine. Uncle Yorek and I will look after you."

And even in the darkness Irena could make out her mother's sad smile.

26.

1945.

In the west there was still bitter fighting between the Allies and the German army. In the concentration camps they continued to exterminate the Jews, but in Eastern Poland, in the Lublin region, life was slowly, slowly returning to normal.

It was hard to believe that everyone lived on the same continent.

Despite the official approval from the authorities, and despite the promises that they would receive help, only a few survivors returned to Parczew. They were gaunt, ashen, their eyes were restless, and they were full of stories of Nazi murdering, looting, rape, and unprecedented abuse. There were almost no children there. Six-year-old Irena would sit on the stone steps and hope that some child her age would arrive. Women were also scarce.

Menachem Ostrovsky was among the survivors. Menachem the carpenter. Not just any carpenter but a craftsman.

Menachem had lost his wife and children when they were taken to Treblinka and had returned to his hometown to start his life over.

He sat in his old house and began to plan his future. Most of all, he wished to build a family. That is what everyone was doing. After they had lost so much, they sought connection, love and intimacy. They did not want to remain alone. Loneliness was more bitter than hell.

Then the rumor spread that a young, beautiful and, most importantly, available woman had arrived in Parczew.

The day after Shurka's arrival, the men began to court her. Most of them were too shy to approach her directly so they sent messengers of their good will or they appealed to Ruska and Yorek.

"What's going on here? Three men already offered themselves, two matchmakers are bothering me, and one already sent a sack of nuts."

"Everyone wants to start a family," Ruska explained.

"You are a beautiful woman," Yorek added. "They say good things about you."

Shurka listened and shook her head. No, the time was not yet right for her. She still missed the man she had lost, still spoke to him in the night. She still felt his hand on her shoulder.

Ruska approached Shurka, "Chiluk Shatz, the town teacher asked me today if he could bring us a cup of tea sometime, and Ezu Bronman from the hat shop asked me if you might want to go for a walk with him tomorrow evening."

Shurka had to stifle her laughter and simply blushed.

"I don't think so... give me time. When the right one comes along I will know immediately," was her consistent reply.

"You are the most courted woman in Parczew," Yorek told her. "The men are awaiting your decision."

"Sure and why not?" Ruska was quick to set things straight. "My sister is the most beautiful woman in the whole region! Let them wait."

Shurka rejected the advances of the tailor, the scholar, the doctor, the partisan, even the owner of the cinema. But when Menachem Ostrovsky showed up one evening, bearing a package wrapped in newspaper, with candlesticks inside, her heart skipped a beat. She knew who he was, knew his family, and secretly hoped that he would also come to see her.

"I brought this for you so you can light the Sabbath candles," said Menachem. He presented the candlesticks to Ruska and stole a glance at Shurka. And remained standing. His eyes were fixed on the floor, as though afraid his true intentions would be discovered.

"Thank you, we actually need candlesticks. We were forced to sell ours..."

Menachem Ostrovsky did not answer. His home was also without the silver candlesticks that had been passed down for generations.

He knew that many people were saved by their silver.

"I have to go," Menachem finally said, but remained standing, as though asking that the visit not come to an end.

"Maybe stay and eat supper with us?" Yorek offered. He hoped that maybe a little miracle would happen and Shurka's heart would open to this man. Ruska noticed her sister's eyes sparkling with a new light. She hurried to set the table for a guest.

"They were right," Shurka recalled, smiling a sweet smile, as though seeing Menachem again for the first time.

That night Menachem dreamed that Shurka stood beneath the tall elms. She gestured for him to follow her and led him to a grove in the woods. There she told him that with neither walls nor roof, this was the home the forest had given her.

"This is where everyone I loved lies. They no longer dream."

In Menachem's dream, Shurka wrapped a scarf around him, took his hand and placed it close to her heart.

He rested his head and heard her low sighs as though something inside her was crying.

A big tear rolled down and wet his leg.

He wanted to tell her that his heart was empty, but she whispered to him that he had always been hers.

"You, Menachem. You're the one."

And he knew then that he would follow her anywhere in the world.

She said, "All of us are lost souls. We were thrown into the depths and sank like leaden soldiers, and only part of us floated back up. We left the others to die."

She gave him her hand and led him slowly.

The sun rose like honey above her.

And the smells of spring filled his soul.

She showed him children and elderly, women and men who had been heartlessly thrown there.

And you will want to move.

For I trust in my soul.

When he awoke he knew that he and Shurka had been destined for each other from above. Sarah, our foremother.

And Shurka?

"This was the first night that I didn't dream of my Avraham," she told Ruska the next morning. "Do you think I am a sinful woman?"

"I think you are a smart and strong woman."

"Menachem Ostrovsky was really the first who appealed to me," she recounted later. "The only one aside from my Avraham, of course. When he came to us and smiled, he seemed like someone I could go on a new journey with - to build, to grow, to rely on. Right away I loved his broad hands, his smooth face, and I thought, why not? One must carry on and build. Let's give it a chance and we'll see."

Menachem was a handsome, strong and courageous man. Vitality burned in his eyes and his smile conveyed a kind of magic. Even after the years he had spent hiding in the forest, even after he had lost his wife and children, he never ceased to be loving and full of life. He was an artisan and the furniture he built was well-regarded all over the region.

On the day after Menachem came to visit, Ruska hinted to Yorek that they should leave the new couple alone. The next day the pair went for a walk. Her hand rested on his arm and they walked slowly beside each other, their faces beaming, as though they had been touched by angels.

"Look, look, our Queen Shurka found herself a king," everyone said, clicking their tongues. The rumor spread like wildfire; a new couple was building their life over in the ruins of Parczew.

When, one month later, Menachem asked for her hand, Shurka did not hesitate for a moment.

"Are you ready? Truly?" Menachem rubbed his hands in embarrassment, hoping he had heard her correctly.

"I wish to marry you, Menachem," Shurka said without hesitation. And he, red-faced and happy, placed a wooden bracelet in her lap that he had carved with his own hands and a wooden clip, painted red, for her hair.

"I'm sorry," he said, "I did not manage to get a gold ring. But you will see, someday I will cover your hands and neck with gold."

"This bracelet is prettier than a thousand diamonds," Shurka put on the wooden bracelet. "I know the love that went into it."

After agreeing to wed in the month of November, and determining all the details of the wedding and the guest list, Shurka asked him to take her and Irena to her parents' home.

Ever since she had arrived in Parczew she had wanted to visit her old village, to see the old house she had grown up in, that still frequented her dreams.

Menachem agreed happily.

He rented a horse and cart, and together with Yorek and Ruska, they all set out on the path leading to the village. They arrived in Wolka Zablocka at midday. Following Shurka's instructions, Menachem stopped at the big junction. Irena ran after her as she got out of the wagon.

The neighbors' house was painted green, with a blue fence around it.

"There!" cried Shurka, "Here is the pole where the storks' nest sits, and there is the pear tree and the broken fence... my father built it... and also there..." But instead of their house, her gaze fell on an empty lot grown wild with weeds. The neighbors' houses were quiet. Nobody came out to greet them, only two dogs barking angrily as if to scare them away.

In great pain, near desperation, the sisters began to turn over the big stones, hoping maybe to find something underneath them, some memento that would prove that a happy family had once lived here.

"Stop," Menachem held her, "you are hurting yourself, let's go."

"Before we left," she explained to him, "we thought we would be back soon, so our father left some jewelry and gold rings behind. We even left some prayer books."

"Leave it be, there's no way we will find it, the Poles ransacked everything."

"Maybe just the Torah books," Shurka said to Ruska. "What would the goyim do with them? I am sure they are here. Maybe if we just dig we will find something, some remnant."

Yorek and Menachem dug and turned over every stone but

they found nothing.

When they finally gave up and set off back to Parczew, the sun was beginning to set. They went for a few minutes without saying a word, each deep in painful memories.

"Don't look back," Shurka said at last, when the village was behind them. "So we won't wind up like Lot's wife. We must only look forward."

"Just like your Avraham taught me," Yorek laughed.

"Like Avraham," Shurka agreed and silence fell.

"Avraham will always be with us, in joy, in sorrow, but look, we are already looking ahead to a better future," Menachem put his arms around his future wife.

One month later, in November of 1944, Menachem Ostrovsky and Shurka were wed.

The small community that had begun to grow in Parczew got together to prepare the wedding party.

Yorek managed to obtain some light-colored curtain fabric from one of his Polish friends, and Shurka and Ruska sewed a wedding dress from it, embroidering white lilies onto the hem. On her head she wore a crown of wild flowers that Irena had picked from the garden in the center of town. And when she walked toward the man who awaited her with a broad smile, Irena by her side holding her dress, her lips murmured her gratitude for the opportunity she had been given to start over anew with a companion.

Later, when Menachem asked her how she had chosen him from all of her many suitors, she answered him simply, "Because of the love I saw in you. When you told me how much you had loved your wife and family, I knew that you knew how to give all of that love that is inside you to us, to your new family."

And to her grandchildren she added years later, "And also because he was the most handsome man in Parczew, and had good hands."

The new couple moved to live in the back room on the ground floor of Menachem's family's house.

And Irena was happy.

Not only did she now hear her mother laughing and singing while she sewed or kneaded dough, but she finally had a room of her own. Sure it was a small room with thin walls, but it was full of light and through the window she could look out at the world outside. She could watch the clearing away of ruins and the feverish building that was taking place all around, and could see the refugees fill the streets of the new Parczew.

Almost a year later, in January 1945, their prince was born.

Their son, Yaakov. Kobi.

27.

The Ostrovsky home in Parczew was a spacious corner house. From one side the Great Church could be seen. On the corner across the street stood a water pump. Farther along, towards the edge of town where the flour mill stood, was a fire department building that had been converted into a movie theater. It was less than a ten minute walk to the place where the Parczew synagogue had once stood which, during the time of the Nazi occupation, had been defiled, looted, destroyed and had also, per German orders, been converted into a cinema.

Behind the house stood the "Olernik," a sunflower oil factory that belonged to the family's grandfather.

Fortunately, when it was ransacked during the war, the looters did not realize the value of the machine that made oil. Even though they had broken it, they had left it in place. Now Menachem decided that it was a good time to reestablish the factory. He set about cleaning the machine and traveled through the neighboring villages to find replacement parts for those that were damaged. The little factory returned to function and provided a nice livelihood for the family as well as some relatives who had joined them in Parczew.

Slowly but surely, life returned to a new normal. During the days, people tried to talk about the prices of vegetables, newly married couples that had or babies that had been born, even about the future, as though the war had never happened.

But at night they were faced with their nightmares, talked to their deceased loved ones and carried their great burden of pain. Nonetheless, in the morning they rose to a new day and everybody hurried about their business. They were the *Sh'erit Hapletah* ("the surviving remnant"). The survivors. All they wanted was to live. They wanted to believe they were free.

Polish Jewry, which had numbered around 5.3 million people before the war, had been almost entirely exterminated.

Between 40,000 and 100,000 total Jews survived the Holocaust. Another 150,000 Jewish refugees returned to Poland after having escaped during the war. But they were not well-received; the first Jewish survivors to return were greeted with outright hostility.

"I don't understand," said Ruska, who now asked everyone to call her Shosh. "Papa always believed that the Jews and Poles were brothers."

"Well, it has become clear that that is not the case," Menachem said. "Their hidden anti-Semitism was aroused and spread by the Nazis. It's plain to me that they do not want us here. The government has no desire to re-assimilate the Jews."

"Hitler evidently understood the true feelings of these people, while my parents mistakenly considered this their homeland," Shurka grieved.

"Your parents were naive - it's no coincidence that Poles handed Jews over to the Germans. Of course there were those who helped Jews, and even we ourselves even found good friends, but the majority... I am worried. It's not a good place to stay."

It was not surprising that when these anti-Semitic feelings grew, it led to new persecutions.

In 1946, the Kielce pogrom took place, during which 42 Jews were killed and 80 wounded out of the 200 Jews in the city. That pogrom was deeply disillusioning to those Holocaust survivors who had hoped to resettle in Polish society.

Parczew was also at risk.

One morning a knock was heard at the door. The only people home at that time were Shurka and Irena and Kobi, who was sleeping in her arms. Shurka hesitated for a moment, but the man called Menachem's name and insisted that she open up. He claimed he had important news.

Shurka sent Irena to her room and called to Yorek. Only then did she open the door.

"Thank God," the stranger said and hurried inside. "Quickly, quickly."

"What happened?"

"I came to warn you all."

"To warn us, from what?"

"Yesterday, when I brought my wares to the market, I heard them speaking..."

"Who did you hear? I don't understand what it is you're talking about. Who are you?"

"Don't be afraid of me, I am a good friend of the Ostrovsky family." The man took off his hat. A patch of his beard was pale and he had many Vitiligo markings all over his skin.

"My name is Sauli Jocko. Menachem and I studied together at the same school. You must be Shurka, his new wife." He stretched out his hand and stroked Kobi's head.

"May he be healthy and strong, like his father."

"Thank you," said Shurka. "Will you come in and drink something?"

"Not today. I just came to deliver the warning. Listen, they plan to kill Jews. You must be careful and warn everybody else."

"But the authorities themselves invited us to return..."

"Please, there's no time to deliberate. Take care of yourselves. And now you must excuse me, I have to go. They can't know that I warned you."

"Maybe you could at least wait for Menachem. He will be back soon..."

"I have to get back. Listen, I don't know when... it could even be tomorrow or the next day, I don't know exactly," said Jocko.

"And what must we do?"

"Warn everyone! Don't go out in the streets - they are waiting for you there," he said and vanished before she had a chance to thank him.

Shurka did not doubt the urgency of the warning. To avoid losing time they packed blankets, clothes, water and food for a few days and waited for Menachem to return. When he learned of the visit he too understood the gravity of the situation. He had heard what was happening in other towns and knew that they did not have much time.

"I must go out," he told his wife. "I don't think they will come tonight." Shurka bit her lip and did not prevent him from leaving. She knew that at these moments they had to think of the community and not just her own family's safety.

Menachem hurried to warn everyone he could about the attack. He recruited more friends to help people find hiding places and to equip themselves with food and medicine.

Ruska and Yorek also went from house to house urging Jews to flee and to find hiding places because hard times were about to come.

When they returned, their faces were flushed from their efforts.

"Shurka," Menachem said, his voice hoarse, "Let's go, we're leaving." He went to wake Irena from her sleep.

"Why?"

"The ground floor is too dangerous - we will be the first to get hurt. We have to move to that other house, the lion house where you lived with your sister before the wedding. We will feel safer on the second floor when those bastards come, and from there we can also keep an eye on them."

Shurka saw resolve in his eyes and knew he was right.

"Let's go," she said encouragingly, "we will do what we must."

The rioters arrived in Parczew in the evening, two days later.

They were looking for Jews to hit, kill, loot. They brought hatred with them.

"Jews have money, they sleep on their gold," they said to anyone who would listen.

They went about the streets of the town with clubs in their hands and fury on their faces.

On the way they met a large man wearing a cap with a visor, pushing a baby carriage. Kobi sat in the stroller, on top of a blanket covering food that Menachem had bought to bring to the families in hiding.

"Where are you headed?" the men surrounded him, their eyes trying to examine his eyes, to find fear.

"I am hurrying to the pharmacy of Jan Valdinevsky," said Menachem.

"And this?" one of them pointed at the stroller. Kobi opened his eyes and smiled at the rioter.

"This is Stefak, my son. He is one and a half."

"What are you doing in the street with a baby, smuggling rifles to Jews? Is that what you're doing? What do you have there under that little Stefak of yours?"

"My wife is sick," Menachem bowed his head. "Her temperature has not gone down in a week and the doctor sent me to bring medicine. She is in bad shape."

"And why is the baby with you and not in his bed?"

"I cannot leave him beside his mother - she is contagious."

"Contagious you say. What is wrong with her?"

"Scarlet fever. We have to get going," and he began to walk away.

His friends hesitated for another moment.

One of them managed to warn him, "I recommend that you return home and don't come out for the next few hours."

"Why?" Menachem asked innocently.

"It might be dangerous in the streets." He hinted to Menachem to get closer and he whispered into his ear. "Do you understand who we are? We came to clean the city of its Jews."

Long afterwards Menachem would tell of the moment where he looked death in the face and was unafraid.

"I felt strong and sure. I felt that if I had survived the war and I was living my life over, I must be invulnerable. Nothing could touch me. Luckily for me our little Yaakov was smart and already at one and a half he understood what was happening and didn't cry. Thanks to scarlet fever that sometimes has its function."

At the same time a decision was formed in his heart.

Enough.

He would not live among the Gentiles. He and his family could not live in fear of being beaten or robbed at any moment. He did not want to be afraid any longer. He would have to join his people in the blooming land of their forefathers.

Menachem did not tell his family about the incident until they were already on board the ship *Kedma* on their way to

Israel. He did not want to add fear on top of fear and worried that this episode would be hard for Shurka to process.

The rampage in the streets of Parczew lasted for four hours and none of the authorities put a stop to it.

Shurka, Irena and baby Yaakov sat huddled together inside a clothes closet in the bedroom for four hours. Menachem stood ready beside the door holding a big hammer in his hands. He was determined to defend his family; he would not let anybody enter.

Even after the gunshots stopped, nobody dared to leave the house. I was not until the following day that they learned the extent of the catastrophe. Three Jews had been killed in the attack.

Avram Zisman, a 40-year-old porter, Yaakov Mendel Turbiner, a 22-year-old bachelor, and David Tampi, a 36-year-old baker, who left behind a wife and a baby girl just a few months old.

The three men had come through one inferno only to be killed in the pogrom after the war.

In the apartment beside Shurka and Menachem's, Yosef Stern and his family hid in the storage space over the ceiling. The Poles turned the place upside down and smashed the furniture but did not find them. Nor did they enter the Ostrovsky family's apartment. Was this a miracle? Destiny? Or, as Menachem said: "God decided that he had abused us enough."

After the dead were buried, after the obituaries and the prayers, it was clear to everyone that Poland was no longer their homeland: Poland was not a safe place for Jews.

They had to get out of there.

Now they thought of going west.

"And there?"

"We will manage. The Jews are gathering in displaced persons camps, waiting to immigrate to Israel."

"How do you know all this?"

"Here, look, I will read to you from the newspaper, 'the Jews that fled Poland arrived in areas held by the Allied forces: DP camps in Germany, Austria and Italy. About 250,000 refugees are living in the camps in crowded conditions. Some of the refugees have even been housed in the newly liberated concentration and extermination camps.'"

"Nothing is as terrible as living in the bunkers."

"It's not so simple my dear Shurka. The Allied armies stationed in Germany and Austria are not so pleased with the Jews immigrating to the west, and they are doing everything they can to close the border. What we have been through isn't enough for them..."

"Who will stand in our way?" laughed Shurka. "We are forest people... nothing will stop us!"

28.

If someone had asked Menachem where he was taking his family he would have answered that he did not know, but that Poland was no longer suitable and they had to get out of there.

Three days after the pogrom, Shurka and Menachem packed up their belongings, hired a horse and wagon and headed for the train station.

Ruska and Yorek set off a week before them; they planned to meet in Lublin.

"Just don't let me lose you," Shurka hugged her sister. "I have already lost too much."

"Never," said Yorek. "And lose my friend Irena?"

"Don't worry. Just to be safe we will leave you messages and instructions with the Jewish community."

"Why Lublin?" asked Shurka after Menachem told them his plans. "We should go someplace where we can settle permanently."

"There's no choice," he said. "We have to leave Parczew. First we will get to Lublin and then we will plan our next steps."

"Where to?"

"To the new homeland."

"They say there is a war there, that they aren't letting Jews move there."

"It's our homeland."

"I want to go to America," said Shurka. She saw America as a promise of a better life.

But Menachem did not want to hear of America.

"I am not willing to live among Gentiles anymore," he insisted. "The time has come for us to live with our brothers, and not at the mercy of others."

"But everyone in America is an immigrant: Poles, Russians, Italians, also Jews."

"Italians, Russians, they're all Gentiles. In the Land of Israel important things are happening."

"I already applied for a permit to go to America."

"So someone else can use you? I am moving to the land of my forefathers, to a house which is mine."

"They say that in America everyone is a millionaire!"

"Enough fairytales. Millionaires are people like us who have their freedom."

"Wouldn't it be better to be a free millionaire?" Shurka laughed before going on. "Who's waiting for us there? You don't know a single soul who lives in that Israel of yours."

"Everyone there is Jewish."

"In America we have friends and relatives."

"Enough talk. First we have to get out of here," Menachem tried to appease her. "In Lublin we will meet the Jewish council with your sister and there we will decide our future."

Menachem did not change his mind even when they met on the eve of their immigration to Israel with his sister Ora in Marseilles. Her attempts to convince them to settle with her in Paris were met with outright refusal.

"Stay with us... Paris is the city of lights," Ora argued. "The whole world dreams of being there."

"We dream of settling the land of Zion," said Menachem.

"And what do you say?" Ora asked Shurka.

"My homeland is with Menachem."

"Your grandfather insisted," Shurka would tell her grandchildren years later. "He wanted to live among his fellow Jews; he was tired of the Gentiles. Grandpa was a Zionist and I was convinced by his faith."

Menachem knew exactly what he wanted.

They tried to figure out how to reach their destination. Lublin was just a station along the way. In the week they spent there, they got organized with money, clothes and travel documents that the council issued for them, and they embarked on their journey west. Just like thousands of other refugees, they too wanted to cross the border into Germany to reach the free American zone.

"And from there?"

"From there we will decide," Menachem told his wife.

Their first station was in the town of Bilba in Lower Silesia, not far from the German border. Before the Second World War, Bilba had been a German city. It was annexed to Poland after the war, along with Wroclaw and other cities in western Poland. The journey from Lublin to Bilba took three days. The schedule, as so often happened in those years, was disrupted. The trains were delayed by many hours, and more than once they were forced to spend the night on the platform, as they waited for a late train. The 450 km trip became an exhausting three-day journey.

Irena was already eight years old and Yaakov was an easy, happy toddler who smiled at everyone and elicited smiles from them in return.

Finally they reached the forest. They got off the train in the early morning hours.

The city had not yet awakened to face the day but one could

see the beauty of the place. They bought tea from one of the peddlers, washed their faces and went left the station. The first thing they saw was the tower of a Gothic church toward which, according to the instructions they had received from Lublin's Jewish council, they were supposed to walk. The office of the Dror Movement, situated just behind it, was still closed, so they sat in one of the area's pretty gardens. After Parczew and Lublin, which had been destroyed during the war, the city was well-preserved. Beautiful buildings from the 18th century ornamented the city center and in addition to the large gardens, there were well-kept shops. They bought themselves fresh bread from the bakery and waited for the office to open.

"Here you are! Where did you disappear to?" called Miriam, a member of the Dror movement, when she arrived at the office an hour later. "We've been looking for you all over town."

"We didn't know," Shurka apologized. "And anyway, how did you know we were supposed to arrive?"

Miriam's face lit up with a smile. "They call it the courageous connection of the Jewish people."

Someone they had met at the previous station who knew Miriam had called her and reported that they were supposed to arrive. An emissary had been sent to wait for them at the train station, but they had passed him by and he had lost them.

"We found them!" Miriam announced to anyone who needed updating and for an hour or so they were surrounded by members of the Dror movement who lavished love and concern upon them.

"We've arranged an apartment for you, with a small yard for the children."

"Are there others like us here?" Shurka asked. "I mean... like we... those who..."

"Yes?"

"Survivors…"

"She means refugees," said Menachem.

"You are not refugees," Miriam hastened to assure them. "There are a number of Jewish families here who spent the war as you did, who came a few weeks ago."

"A few weeks ago? And they're still here?" Menachem asked, amazed. "Why? We thought we'd be able to cross the border next week."

"Patience, friends, it's not so simple," said the man who was introduced to them as Yossi, the *shaliach*, a representative from Israel.

"What is he saying?" Menachem and Shurka tried to understand.

"He speaks Hebrew. He said you must be patient," Miriam translated to them.

"Ask him what we have to do in order to leave Poland."

"To wait," answered Yossi. "We are taking care of everything, don't worry."

"We have no patience left. We used it all up in the war."

"There is no alternative."

The bright little apartment they were given had belonged until not long before, to a German family that had escaped from the threat of occupation. Cheese and fresh vegetables were waiting for them and they began to believe that the world could be good to them again.

"We must be patient," Menachem repeated what Yossi the *shaliach* had said, as though trying to reassure himself. "In the meantime we can travel around and see this fine city."

But he and Shurka were impatient anyway. They wanted to get to America already.

"What's the rush?" Yossi asked them and Miriam translated.

"We want to leave here before the winter comes, before the snow."

While Shurka and Irena were walking Yaakov around the old city, picking wild berries around their house and getting to know the neighbors, Menachem routinely patrolled the Dror movement offices. He admired the young people who had come from Eretz Israel. They were tanned, upright and self-confident. They did not look like the Jews he knew... there was something different about them.

"Maybe," he explained to Shurka when she asked him, "it's because they often smile and laugh and start singing for no reason. Soon we will be like that too."

"We said that we will see."

"I already know I will only go to Eretz Israel. It is my place and my people."

And Shurka understood that she would follow him... "Wherever your home will be will be my home as well."

As time passed, Shurka got used to the idea of moving to Israel and gave up her dream of going to America. She knew that Menachem was determined, that he saw the idea of living in the homeland as existentially significant.

"I am happy," Menachem hugged her, "You will see - you won't be sorry."

When she had met a few Israelis, heard their songs and their stories, she appreciated that one day she would speak Hebrew like Miriam and Tzila, the leaders who were teaching her and Menachem and Irena their language.

The months dragged on and their patience began to wane. When they were beginning to lose hope that they would be able to cross the border before snow arrived, Miriam and a young man they had never met before came to their house one evening.

"Itzik," the young man introduced himself, shook their hands and smiled. "What a nice home you have."

"Itzik has come to speak with you about Irena," Miriam explained. Irena heard her name and approached the table.

"What about Irena?" Shurka was taken aback.

"We want the best for you, so we have come to suggest something," said Itzik and Miriam translated. And so it was suggested to them that Irena set off before them. "We send the children first, so Irena would get to Israel before you with a group of child refugees."

"We should let her go alone?"

"Just temporarily, you must understand, crossing the border is against the law, but when it is children without parents, it is easier for us: the authorities allow passage. So it is easier to leave here in stages. First she will go, then you will arrive after."

"When?"

"As soon as it is possible - trust us."

"I don't want..." Irena buried her face in her mother's lap. "What if you don't find me?"

Shurka and Menachem were stunned and also worried. The idea of separating from Irena was hard. After everything they had been through? But Itzik did not understand - he was convinced that this was in everyone's best interest.

"It is easier for children to cross the border and we will get you across afterwards," he reiterated.

"I kept her safe with me for four years... I am not willing to lose her too!"

Shurka and Menachem struggled with this for three days. They did not know what to do or whom to believe. Their hearts were full of doubt but these youth from Eretz Israel were so eager to help them and so sure of themselves.

"You only have two more days to think," Miriam informed them. "Then they are gathering the children and whoever does not come..."

Another sleepless night passed. Shurka and Menachem discussed and considered and in the morning they decided... one fate for all of us. They would not separate. The following day Menachem returned to the office and gave their answer.

"You don't understand..." Yossi tried to change their minds.

"We understand very well, Irena is not ready for that kind of separation."

"That is how she will grow independent. It is for her own good."

"It is for her own good to be with us. Nobody else could understand what that child has been through - she needs us."

"Look at the other children; many parents have given their permission."

"Everybody has their own story. Irena is staying with us."

After three months of being delayed again and again, Menachem decided that enough was enough. They had waited plenty. He assumed that nobody was coming back to get them, that they had been forgotten. Maybe Israel had just wanted Irena but not them, sad refugees after a terrible war.

He knew that there were "*machers*" in the area, people who, in exchange for a sum of money, would be willing to help them over the border. Along with three other Jewish families who were also fed up with waiting, they agreed on a deal with the smugglers and in the middle of the night, without telling anyone anything, they got onto a truck that was waiting for them on the outskirts of town.

The instruction was clear, to remain quiet and obey orders. Menachem did not tell Shurka that there had been instances of *machers* betraying and abandoning their passengers. He did not want her to worry. Yaakov slept in his arms as they got down near a barbed wire fence. A moment later they were already on the other side. Their feet walked on free land.

This time Shurka held back and looked upon her old homeland. It was an especially dark night and heavy clouds hung in the sky. She could not even see the lights of the nearby villages. But for a moment the moon came out from behind the clouds and lit up the hills around, allowing her a parting glance.

"Come, my darling," Menachem lifted her into the air for a moment, then set her down and said, "Breathe deeply, we did it!"

The smugglers from the Polish side disappeared quietly and left them in the darkness. Had they fallen into some sort of trap? Would the border guards be after them right away? Several fearful minutes passed until Menachem pulled himself together and told everyone to lie down on the ground and not speak. He tried to be confident and positive. A few minutes later, a beam of light was seen approaching through the darkness. A smiling face emerged and they were helped to board a truck to the next city.

The way was long. The truck rattled from side to side on the dirt roads they were forced to take to avoid attracting any attention from the police. They didn't stop until the break of day. They were not far from the Dresden railway station, where two of the smugglers were waiting for them, demanding additional payment beyond what had already been paid to bribe the railway officials. Menachem took it upon himself to manage the negotiations and threatened to turn the smugglers in to the authorities. They in turn threatened to turn the refugees in to the police. After fighting and shouting, they shook hands and only then did the smugglers give them coffee and sandwiches and train tickets. They got onto the train heading to Ulm, the first station in liberated Germany.

"You wouldn't believe who was born here in Ulm," laughed Menachem.

"Who? Who?" asked Shurka, sensing his happiness and wanting to join in.

"Albert Einstein, in 1879. The most famous German - and Jewish!"

They stopped in the city where the Danube River passed through, in order to stock up on food and water and discovered that it, along with so many other places, had also been destroyed by Allied bombing.

Their next stop was the displaced persons camp in Leipheim, near Munich, where hundreds of Jewish refugees had gathered and been housed in buildings that used to serve the German air force. In the camp there was a local office for UNRWA - the United Nations Relief and Works Agency, which assisted refugees in finding food and work and provided medical services as well.

It was crowded in the camp. The stream of refugees wanting to move from Poland to Germany was growing but Eretz Israel was controlled by the British and despite all the efforts of the Central Committee, it did not open its gates to survivors.

After a few hard months and the worsening of conditions, it was decided to transfer some of the residents to a more comfortable DP camp in Heidenheim, which was considered to be a desirable tourism destination because of its pretty view

with thick forests and flowing streams. But for Shurka and
Menachem it was just another stop on their long journey. It
never occurred to them that they would stay in this camp for
over two years.

29.

In the ninth month of their stay at the Heidenheim camp, Shurka and Menachem received a message from Ruska. She and Yorek had left Parczew several days before them and had arrived in the American sector of Berlin. From there they moved to another camp in West Germany.

"When you meet me, don't call me Ruska, I'm Shosh and Yorek is Yair... that's how they know us here."

30.

The Ostrovsky family stayed in Heidenheim for two years.

Menachem continued to build furniture with his skilled carpenter's hands, fixing things that had broken, and making the children happy with the wooden toys he invented for them. Shurka received a sewing machine from the camp management, and once more her hands raced across fabrics. In time she became friends with their next door neighbor.

Dorka Gottlieb and her family who had survived the Nazis by the skin of their teeth, had escaped Germany to Russia, and on their way to Israel they too had arrived at the camp.

She had one son, Menashe.

One day in May, 1948, when the smell of spring filled the camp, a shout was heard.

"Jews! Listen, we have a celebration today!"

What happened? Who shouted? People started coming out of all the huts to the street, trying to understand what the brouhaha was about.

Suddenly one of the young people climbed up onto the roof of his hut, raised a blue and white flag and declared, "We have a country - long live the State of Israel!"

Thus the residents of the camp learned that David Ben Gurion, unafraid, had declared the establishment of a country for the Jews - the State of Israel.

"We have a country!"

"We have a homeland!"

Hand joined hand and they formed a large circle of people who only an hour earlier had looked like haunted shadows, who just yesterday had felt extinguished and desperate. Now their eyes were shining and they were singing to the land of their forefathers, facing forward to the rising sun - once again eastward - feeling as though they were all brothers.

People swung their children up onto their shoulders, hugged one another, danced and sang.

"We can hold our heads up high, we have a land of our own."

The camp's residents believed the time had come and they could finally pack up their belongings and move to the land of their forefathers, to realize the great dream.

"But it is still impossible to go," the messengers told them.

"Wait a little longer," they explained.

"It's not yet time," they repeated.

How could that be? It was said that Ben Gurion promised that the new country would be open to any Jew.

They heard his booming voice again and again, proclaiming, "We declare the establishment of the home of the Jews, the State of Israel."

If so then who would prohibit their entry?!

But despite their happiness, they had to continue to wait.

Israel was not yet ready for them.

The newspapers wrote that all the Arab armies had invaded the country and were threatening to expel the Jews. The radio reported bloody battles in places whose names sounded strange to their ears.

They were patient. They knew that they had to wait, not rush. They could only hope that Israel's war for freedom would end quickly and that they could soon arrive on its shores to begin to build the country. When the battles finally ended, and the ceasefire agreements had been signed, the families at last began to leave the camp.

"One more week," Menachem said one day when he arrived home. "That's it, we've done it!"

"What?"

"We're getting out of here. It's all arranged."

"A week? How will we get organized in a week?" Shurka asked.

"You can't manage it in a week?" he hugged her. "Woman, woman... you wait two years to get out of here and now you're complaining?"

"There is so much to be done. To pack, to ship the little furniture that we received from the camp management, to part from friends, and where will we get boxes?"

"It will be alright. Take as little with you as possible, and definitely not that heavy wool coat. In Israel there are heatwaves - soon you will know them all too well."

"What is a heatwave?" Irena asked.

"It's when it is hot for fifty days at a time, hot like you've never felt."

"Better than the Polish cold."

"When there is a heatwave, the snow doesn't fall?" Irena was surprised.

"In the new land there is no snow. We can even swim in the sea in the winter."

For seven days Menachem and Shurka prepared... packing, selling what they could not take with them or leaving it with the friends who were staying behind, parting from friends with fond wishes to meet again someday.

On the last night of their stay at the camp, people arrived

at their house. It seemed that all the camp residents staying behind had come to bid them farewell.

"Write to us," they asked.

"Of course."

"And if possible, let us know how you are doing over there. How the weather is, if it is possible to make a living, and where is the best place to live."

"We are going to live in the desert," laughed Menachem.

"In the desert? I thought we were going to live beside the sea."

"Desert, sea, whatever we want... it's our country."

"They say that you can swim in the sea in Tel Aviv even in winter. That they have the prettiest girls in the world."

"I already have the prettiest one," Menachem hugged Shurka.

He told them he would be a carpenter in the Land of Israel and would make nice furniture that would make people happy, and Shurka would grow orange trees in their garden and maybe watermelon and green onions, and in the evenings she would read stories to the children.

"And sometimes she will even have time to look after her husband," Menachem winked at Shurka.

Everyone nodded their heads eagerly.

Menachem was capable of anything and could be counted on. He was solid as a rock. Since they had been together, Shurka no longer tossed and turned at night but slept peacefully in his warm embrace.

It was no wonder that when they set sail for the Land of Israel on the *Kedma*, and little Yaakov asked to get off the ship - the rocking from the waves made him ill - but the doctor said it was impossible - there was only water in every direction, there was no place to get off.

"Why impossible?"

"That's how it is."

"Call my father."

"And what will your father do?" the doctor laughed.

"My father is Menachem the carpenter, he never says anything is impossible."

"And what will he do?"

"My father has high boots up to his knees and he can take us and cross the water no problem, because he can do anything."

The Gottlieb family was among those who came to visit before they left. Dorka Gottlieb presented Shurka Ostrovsky with a box of cookies that she had made.

"For the journey."

"Perfect," said Shurka. "I will take them with me to the Land of Israel. And what about you? When will you join us?"

"Soon. We are next in line."

"When you get there, don't forget to look for us."

"How will we know where to find you?"

"Very simple. When you get off at the port of Haifa, ask where Shurka the beautiful lives and everyone will know immediately," laughed Menachem.

"Menachem, Menachem, what will we do with you? You're always joking," Shurka blushed.

"You're lucky," whispered Dorka. "To live with a happy man is a gift."

Shurka hugged her. She knew that Moshe, Dorka's husband, never smiled. He wore a deep sadness on his face. Before the war he had been first violin in the Royal Polish Orchestra, but he had lost a hand in the war and would never be able to play again.

"But you can teach."

"Yes, but I don't know if they're looking for violin teachers in the new country."

"Don't worry," said Menachem. "You will have plenty of work."

"After we arrive," Shurka promised, "we will write you as soon as we're organized. You will get a page full of instructions and tips."

A few months later the Gottlieb family boarded the ship *Galila* and went to Israel. The two families found each other and the camaraderie that had begun in the camp was renewed. Moshe indeed found work teaching violin and his name spread through the country as a popular and beloved teacher.

Shurka and Menachem were keenly aware that this was their last night at the camp and that the final leg of their journey to the Land of Israel would begin in the morning. Neither could manage to sleep. Each of them saw their lives pass before their eyes, the route and the transformation they had had to go through in order to stand at the gateway to freedom. This was in many ways a difficult separation - both were leaving behind loved ones buried in the earth of Europe - but they knew they were right to make this move.

To start over again.

One more step and that's it, prayed Menachem.

On a cold December morning, they woke the children, brought them a hot cup of tea and a jam sandwich. For the last time, they passed through the little kitchen to the balcony of the apartment that had been their temporary home for two and a half years, and went out to wait for the truck. Shurka and Yaakov sat beside the driver, a burly German who did not stop talking about how much he loved the Jews and how much he hated the Nazis who had destroyed his country.

"Now everybody loves us," Shurka said in Polish.

"Just wait. Anti-Semitism isn't dead, just dormant," predicted Menachem.

"I hope to God you are mistaken."

Menachem and Irena got in the back of the truck and were able to watch the camp disappear behind the snowy mountains.

At the train station, the German driver helped them load their bundles and a messenger from Israel hugged them and handed them their tickets.

"This is for you," he handed Irena a golden fruit.

"What is it?"

"It is a fruit that you will only find in our Land of Israel."

"I know what it is!" Shurka jumped in. "It's a golden apple, an 'orange'!"

"How did you know?" Menachem asked.

"How? That's a long story..."

A station and another station. A train and another train. And another. They covered hundreds of kilometers.

"Marseilles," Irena read, "we are in Marseilles."

A truck picked them up from the train station and took them into Marseilles city center. The messenger who was waiting for them explained that tomorrow, two days hence at the latest, they would sail to Haifa. Haifa, the port city of Israel.

"You promise?"

"Absolutely."

"Not two months maybe three?"

"Two days at the most."

"We can't wait any longer," Shurka explained.

Through the window of the small hotel they could see the

ships. The sweet scent of the sea wafted their way.

"Here is the port!" Irena shouted excitedly.

Menachem lifted Yaakov and showed him: "You see there? That is the ship waiting for us, the *Kedma*."

"So small?"

"Small and fast," Menachem laughed. "A ship of smart Jews."

"What does 'Kedma' mean?" asked Yaakov, whose curiosity knew no bounds.

"'Kedma' means eastward," Irena explained. "You understand? Tomorrow we will travel eastward, toward the east, to Eretz Israel!"

Epilogue

When Grandma Sarah reached the age of ninety, her family threw a big celebration. She sat in the place of honor that they had prepared for her, surrounded by loving family, children and grandchildren, brides and grooms, friends and neighbors.

"Tell me, Grandma," one of her grandsons asked, "What was the forest to you?"

"The forest?" Shurka's gaze wandered as though she had returned to the Parczew Forest. "What was the forest to me... on the one hand it was a deadly forest, the cemetery for most of my family but," a smile lit up her face, "the forest was also a lifeline, my bodyguard, it saved me. The forest protected me and my child.

Then she hugged her loved ones, "The forest will forever be in my heart."

This is the story of the life of Sarah.

Sarah, whose loved ones called her "Shurka."

She was smart and beautiful like our foremother, Sarah.

This is the story of one woman who went through hell.

It is a story of love and loyalty, heroism and rebirth, a story of the love of life and a rare and special woman. A woman of light.

Hers is each our story.